Family Business II

Book 2

A Sword of Division

Family Business Series

Family Business II

A Sword of Division

Vanessa
Miller

Book 2
Family Business Series

Vanessa Miller

www.vanessamiller.com

Printed in the United States of America
© 2016 by Vanessa Miller

Praise Unlimited Enterprises
Charlotte, NC

4

Anthologies (Editor)
Keeping the Faith
Have A Little Faith
This Far by Faith

EBOOKS
Love Isn't Enough
A Mighty Love
The Blessed One (Blessed and Highly Favored series)
The Wild One (Blessed and Highly Favored Series)
The Preacher's Choice (Blessed and Highly Favored Series)
The Politician's Wife (Blessed and Highly Favored Series)
The Playboy's Redemption (Blessed and Highly Favored Series)
Tears Fall at Night (Praise Him Anyhow Series)
Joy Comes in the Morning (Praise Him Anyhow Series)
A Forever Kind of Love (Praise Him Anyhow Series)
Ramsey's Praise (Praise Him Anyhow Series)
Escape to Love (Praise Him Anyhow Series)
Praise For Christmas (Praise Him Anyhow Series)
His Love Walk (Praise Him Anyhow Series)
Could This Be Love (Praise Him Anyhow Series)
Song of Praise (Praise Him Anyhow Series)

Prologue

Demetrius and Angel Shepherd laid on the beach gazing into each other's eyes. They had said 'I do' just two days ago and were now enjoying a week-long vacation in the Bahamas; compliments of Don Shepherd, Demetrius' father.

"I wish we could stay here forever," Angel told her husband as he wrapped his arms around her and pulled her close.

"I can see why. It's beautiful here."

"It's not just the beauty," Angel told him. "It seems so peaceful here. There's no body pulling on you, expecting things that you shouldn't be doing. And there's no body pulling on me, expecting me to be something I'm probably never going to be."

Demetrius planted a kiss on his wife's forehead. He knew that she was still upset with her mother for questioning whether or not the two of them belonged together. After their wedding, Angel had pulled him aside and told him that her mother was worried about them; something about the bible saying, 'How can two walk together if they do not agree'. But, Demetrius had told her right then and there, that they didn't have a problem, because no two people on the face of the earth could be more suited for each other. He lifted her head to face him as he told her again, "We are perfect for each other,

Angel. You don't have to worry about us. If I don't know anything, I know that God sent you to me. We're meant to be."

Smiling she said, "Even though our upbringing was totally different? And the fact that my parents are preachers doesn't bother you anymore?"

Demetrius waved the thought off. "That's their life. They can stay in North Carolina, preaching the Gospel and calling down angels on as many people as they want. They have nothing to do with the way we live back in Ohio."

"What about your daddy?" Angel questioned. "I don't like the fact that everything we have comes through him. Why can't you just get a regular job? I know you can't play baseball anymore, but you could coach, right?"

He leaned away a bit, still looking into her eyes. "Oh so now that you've got the ring, you all of a sudden have a problem with the way I make a living?"

"It's not that, Demetrius. I know who you are and how good of a heart you have. I just worry that I might lose you. And I couldn't bare being without you."

Demetrius pulled himself out of the lounge chair, picked Angel up and ran down towards the ocean with her.

"Don't you dare, Demetrius. I don't have on a swim cap and I just got my hair done."

Demetrius wasn't trying to hear it. He threw her in the water and then jumped in behind her. She flapped one arm while trying to wipe the ocean water from her face with the other. When Demetrius reached her, he grabbed hold of the flailing arm. "Calm down woman. I got you."

"You shouldn't have thrown me in here."

"I had to. I need to show you something."

"But you know I can't swim that good."

Demetrius didn't respond. He just wrapped one arm around Angel and stroked the water with the other arm. They rode the wave that came upon them, and then drifted all the way back to the beach. Just as Angel began to relax, they slid into the wet sand. Instead of lifting her out of the water, Demetrius put both arms around her and let the back of her head sink into the sand as he kissed her over and over again.

Angel forgot about her hair as she basked in the love that she had found. "I love you, boo."

He kissed her again, then lifted her from the sand. "I love you too. See how I kept you safe in the water?"

Angel nodded.

"So, don't you ever doubt that I'm going to always be right here, by your side, keeping you safe."

"We'll be together forever, even if we have to go back to the real world and deal with our families, right?" Angel looped an arm around Demetrius' arm as they walked back

"Nothing and nobody is going to split us up. They already tried and failed. So, that's the end of their story... but ours is just beginning."

Demetrius and Angel made all sorts of promises to each other during their glorious honeymoon. Saul, the angel that had been charged with bringing this union together for the child who would be born to save a generation from their sins. watched the two love birds with sadness in his eyes.

Angels rarely shed tears, but Saul's heart was bleeding for Angel and Demetrius. The two loved each other so much, but their love would be sorely tested, and the child's life would be in jeopardy before any ministry would go forth. Demetrius towel dried Angel's hair and wiped the sand off of her as he planted kiss after kiss on her neck. Angel was giggling and all seemed right with the world. But yet and still, a single tear drop fell from Saul's face and hit the sand as he walked away from them. He had to journey back to heaven, and would not be called upon again, until their started falling apart.

One

Give ear O my people, to my law: incline your ears to the words of my mouth. I will open my mouth in a parable: I will utter dark sayings of old. Which we have heard and known, and our fathers have told us.
We will not hide them from their children, showing to the generation to come the praises of the Lord, and his strength, and his wonderful works that he hath done. For he established a testimony in Jacob, and appointed a law in Israel, which he commanded our fathers, that they should make them known to their children:
That the generation to come might know them, even the children which should be born; who should arise and declare them to their children. That they might set their hope in God, and not forget the works of God, but keep his commandments.
Psalm 78: 1-7

Ten years after the honeymoon... 1991

"Wake up, Demetrius, it's time." Angel elbowed her husband in the back and shoved him.

Falling off the bed, Demetrius jumped up, raced around the room looking for her suitcase, and then he turned to Angel and asked, "Where's your bag?"

"What bag?"

"The bag for the hospital. Come on, I thought you said it's time."

Angel threw the covers off, as she laughed at her husband. "Yeah, it's time for you to get the kids ready for school."

It took Demetrius a moment, but he scratched his head, looked around one last time and then said, "I must have been dreaming. I thought you were pregnant and that we had to get to the hospital."

"Sounds more like a nightmare to me. Because if you get me pregnant again," she stood up and took a boxer's stance as she punched at the air, "I'll have to fight you."

He shimmied over to her. "Girl, you know you want to carry another one of my kids in that snap-back belly of yours." He rubbed her stomach, which was indeed flat, as if she hadn't already been pregnant three times.

When she and Demetrius got together, Angel already had a son, DeMarcus. Since DeMarcus' father was a bum and a loser, Demetrius adopted him right after they were married and changed his last name to Shepherd. DeMarcus had been three at the time. Before DeMarcus' fifth birthday, Angel gave birth to Demetrius Jr., whom they all call Dee.

When Dee turned three, Angel gave birth to Dontae. She expected to be giving birth to another child when Dontae turned three, but it didn't happen. Dontae would be five in two days, and Angel had her hands full with DeMarcus' football practice, Dee was having trouble in school and Dontae had fallen in love with baseball and wanted nothing more than to take over his father's baseball

11

dreams. So, she was tired, and had decided that enough was enough. "I can't have any more kids, Demetrius."

He shook his head. "That's not going to work. We still don't have a little girl. And our house will not be complete until we have her."

"Too bad WE don't have to have her, or chauffeur her around and help with the homework. All of that's on ME. And honey, I love you to pieces, but I'm tired."

"I'm helping." He walked over to the bed and lifted the covers. "Get back in bed. Take a good long nap. I'll get the kids dressed myself, and drive them to school. Then I'll be back here with breakfast."

Angel put a hand on Demetrius' cheek. Life with him had been more wonderful than she had dreamed. He provided for her in every way. They lived in a five bedroom home in a quiet neighborhood. She didn't fear for her children when they went out to play, and that in and of itself took a load off of her mind. "I appreciate everything you've done for us, Bae. No one could be a better husband or father than you. But I'm not built for this. I really think three kids is my limit. So, please stop having dreams about pregnant women; or I'm going to wonder if you're cheating on me. Okay?"

Ignoring her comments, Demetrius asked, "Are you going to get back in this bed and let me spoil you or should I just go back to sleep and let you handle everything yourself?"

He didn't have to ask her again, she hopped back in bed, and lifted the covers over her head before he could renege on his promise of giving her a day off.

"Are you comfortable now? Are you relaxed?"

As an answer to her husband's questions Angel pretended to snore.

Demetrius walked out of their bedroom laughing at her antics. But he was in no way done with their conversation. Angel thought she had too much on her hands to even consider having another child. But Demetrius desperately wanted to add a beautiful little girl to their family circle. He knew exactly what Angel needed, and after dropping the kids off, he was going to make sure she got it.

Demetrius wasted little time in getting his sons out of bed and off to school. Dontae was attending a half-a-day pre-school, so he would have to be picked back up by 1 pm. But in between that time, Demetrius drove over to Riverview and Broadway and pulled into the parking lot of the drive-thru that his father owned.

Demetrius had been running this business, a laundromat, cleaners and a grocery store ever since Dee had been born. His Dad had purchased the businesses to launder the money he and his partners were making from all the drugs being smuggled into the city. And Don graciously provided his son with a healthy income while allowing him to be a businessman, in theory… rather than the dope man. But it was all pretty much the same thing, since Demetrius knew where the money was being funneled to and through. He also knew a whole lot more than that. None of which he discussed with his wife over dinner at night. She was just happy that he was earning a good living in a suit and tie, and she was able to tell her parents that she was married to a businessman.

"Hey Demetrius, I thought you were playing Mr. Mom today?" Tony, his day manager said as he headed for the small office in the front of the building.

"I'm looking for KeKe. I thought she was on the schedule to work today."

"She is," Tony agreed. Then pointed toward the women's bathroom. "She's in there cleaning up. She'll be out in a minute."

KeKe James' mother had been on heroin and her grandmother had been an alcoholic. KeKe had only been fourteen when crack first came to town, even so, she gravitated to it like a moth to a flame. Within the last two years, she'd managed to kick the habit, and Demetrius had given her a job at the drive-thru. He liked KeKe and wanted her to make the changes necessary to get her kids out of foster care. But working around all the beer and wine being sold out of this drive-thru couldn't be good for her long term.

So, Demetrius decided he was going to take care of two problems at once. The bathroom door opened and KeKe came strolling out dragging a trash bag full of her clothes behind her. "Hey Demetrius." She waved at him. "Can I leave my bag in your office?"

"You got put out again?" Demetrius shook his head. He didn't know how KeKe stayed clean with all the drama she dealt with on the regular.

"I didn't have a choice. I had to leave. My cousin started dating one of the dope boys that used to sell me crack. And he tried to give me a couple of bags free to get me hooked again."

"You know you won't get your kids back if you drop dirty urine?"

"Duh, Demetrius. Why you think I'm carrying a trash bag around. I'd rather live on the street than go back on that stuff."

Demetrius had planned to offer KeKe a day job, doing work around the house to help Angel out. But if Angel didn't object, maybe KeKe could take the extra bedroom downstairs and be available for Angel whenever she needed her. "I came here to offer you another job. And since your homeless, I might have a room for you as well."

KeKe's eyes brightened. "What's the job?"

14

Hands in his pockets. "Angel's getting worn out with the kids and all their activities, so I'm looking for a housekeeper. We've got an extra room downstairs, so if Angel is okay with it, then you could be a live-in housekeeper. That way you can save your paycheck so you can get a place of your own... probably even get your kids back."

"And you would do that for me... I mean, trust me in your house like that?"

"Of course I do. You ain't faking it, KeKe. You're for real with it."

Tears sprang to her eyes as she said, "Dang, Demetrius. I ain't never had nobody talking like they believe in me."

"So are you going to take the job, or keep carrying around that trash bag and washing up in any bathroom you can find?"

"Are you kidding?" She threw her bag at Demetrius. "Can I start today?"

~~~~

The smell of pancakes and bacon cooking in her kitchen jolted Angel out of her sleep. She stretched and yawned and then got out of the bed. Angel slid on her house shoes. She then put on her housecoat, because she didn't like walking around a house full of little boys with some of the revealing night gowns that Demetrius bought for her.

Her stomach was growling as she headed downstairs. "Why didn't you wake me up when you came back home?" Angel asked as she headed to the kitchen.

But instead of Demetrius answering her, KeKe popped her head out of the kitchen. "Good morning, Angel."

Angel tightened the rope on her housecoat. "Good morning KeKe. What are you doing here?"

15

"Demetrius told me to get your breakfast done. I hope you like what I fixed. I'm not much of a cook… never had nobody to teach me, but I can fry some bacon and flip some jacks."

Angel liked KeKe. She'd had a rough go of it. Her family seemed more interested in additions than training their kids for survival in this world. Angel had met KeKe over a year ago outside of the drive-thru that Demetrius' father owned. She had come to beg for a job. Demetrius was about to dismiss her, but Angel could tell that this girl needed a break. Before Demetrius could turn her away, Angel said, "I think you should give her a chance."

Angel sat down and laughed. "When Demetrius told me he was going to take care of breakfast, I thought he was going to bring back some pancakes from McDonalds. But then I started smelling food."

"You might want to give him a call," KeKe told her while taking the bacon out of the skillet.

Angel wanted to know what Demetrius was trying to pull, so she grabbed the phone and called her husband's cell. He answered on the second ring. "Hey baby, I'm on my way back. I just ran to the store to grab you some strawberries for your pancakes."

"What are you doing, Demetrius? Why is KeKe cooking in my kitchen?"

"I hired her."

"I know you hired her. I'm the one who told you to give her that job. But that doesn't explain why she's here."

"No, baby, I mean I hired her to be our housekeeper."

"You did what?" Angel exploded.

"You heard me, woman. And don't start complaining. You do a lot around the house and with the kids. I'm trying to give you some help so you won't be so overwhelmed."

16

"Whatever, Demetrius. You ain't slick. I know what this is about." Angel hung up the phone. Her husband wanted her pregnant again so bad that he would hire a housekeeper without discussing it with her first. She went back to the kitchen getting ready to tell KeKe that her services weren't needed.

But KeKe was crying, so Angel rushed over to her. "What's wrong?"

"I burnt your pancakes. I'm so sorry. I wanted to impress you, because I really need this job."

Angel handed KeKe some tissue to wipe her face and blow her nose. "You have a job down at the drive-thru, KeKe. You don't need this job."

KeKe shook her head. "I've been sleeping outside for the past few days, but Demetrius said I could stay in the spare bedroom if I got this job."

"He didn't tell me that." Angel wanted to throttle her husband for putting her in this position.

KeKe was hiccupping as she tried to stop crying. "He told me I would have to talk to you about that. But I was hoping that if you liked my cooking and cleaning that you would let me stay, because this is the only way I'll be able to save enough money to get my own place and then get my kids back."

Well dang. Angel sat back down at the table and said, "I'll take a bacon sandwich. The hot sauce is in the cabinet."

KeKe fixed the sandwich, handed it to Angel and then pulled up a chair next to her. She sat there, staring, waiting for Angel to take a bite.

"KeKe, it's just bacon. I'm sure it's fine."

"But is it good enough to get me this job?"

Demetrius had put her in a no win situation. How could she deny KeKe a job that would help her get her kids back? And if she had help around the house, how could she deny Demetrius the little girl he'd been dreaming of?

Two

Angel had initially objected to KeKe being a live-in housekeeper/nanny, and had only agreed to it because she wanted to help KeKe out. But a month into the arrangement and Angel was thanking her lucky stars that Demetrius had been wise enough to hire KeKe.

Even though Angel was still running the kids all over town for soccer, football and basketball practice, then helping with homework, and then making sure that she was all put together and lovely for when her husband arrived home; she wasn't as tired as she used to be.

KeKe couldn't cook worth a lick, so Angel was still handling all the cooking for the family; but KeKe kept the house clean and tidy. Angel was able to sleep in twice a week as KeKe got the kids ready for school and then Demetrius dropped them off. She and Demetrius had even started having date nights again.

Since KeKe had Saturday and Sunday off, Demetrius and Angel either went to the movies or out to dinner on Friday nights. But tonight, Angel decided that she wanted a little more quiet time with her husband. So she fried some chicken and then packed a picnic basket for two.

Demetrius drove them to a wilderness park. They got out and walked the trail, holding hands and talking. Every once and a while they would stop walking so Demetrius could bend down and kiss her.

"I can't believe how different these last few weeks have been for us," Angel told him. "I have to admit. Even though we only have three children, I was becoming a bit overwhelmed."

"I noticed."

"You did? Wow… I thought I was holding it down."

Demetrius shook his head. "You were getting cranky and that's not your personality. So, I knew that you couldn't handle one more thing on your plate."

Angel was getting emotional. "I started to wonder if something was wrong with me. I mean, I don't work outside of the home like a lot of other women have to do. So, why was it so difficult for me to handle you and three boys?"

"Don't cry baby." He wiped the tears from her face. "You are a wonderful wife and mother. I wouldn't want anyone else raising my kids… And I make enough money for you to stay home. So, that's what we're going to do, because I don't trust any and everybody with our kids."

Angel knew that first-hand, which was the reason that she and Demetrius had stopped going on dates. Demetrius wouldn't approve most of the people she'd lined up to babysit. But even with all the problems KeKe had through the years, they trusted her with the kids. She was good people.

"I'm glad we're able to be together like this. We haven't had much alone time since we started having all these kids," Angel said as she put a strawberry in Demetrius's mouth, and then took the rest

20

of the food she had packed out of the basket and spread it on top of the basket.

"Yeah, we need time for ourselves, Baby. But don't make it seem like I'm over here getting you pregnant every year. We've got three babies, not a dozen."

She held up a hand. "Okay, you're right. But those three boys jump around and break so much stuff, that sometimes it seems like there's a dozen of them."

Demetrius took a bite of his chicken, licked his lips and said, "Now, what you need is a beautiful little girl... that would calm the house down."

"There you go. Just let me enjoy not being so tired all the time for a little while, before you start lobbying for another baby."

Demetrius leaned over and kissed her. "You're right, Bae. Tonight is about me and you. Now feed your man some dinner."

"Oh, so you want me to feed you, huh?" Angel opened the container of baked beans, scooped out a spoonful and then fed it to Demetrius.

"Mmm, that's good. You're the best cook in town. We should open a restaurant."

"Look at you, trying to put more work on my back. Doubt if you'll get more kids like that," Angel joked.

"Hey you two, I didn't know y'all liked nature."

Demetrius looked up. Mo was standing there with his new wife, Tara. He and Mo hadn't worked together since Al and Don beat him so bad that he needed medical attention. Mo was now working for Frankie Day, and even though Demetrius hated the guy, he didn't hold it against Mo. The man had to feed his family. "What you doing out here? I know you're fat self ain't about to walk that trail."

Mo patted his stomach. "Tara wants me to lose some weight."

"Well y'all are more than welcome to join us before your walk. We have a few extra pieces of chicken, some potato salad and bake beans."

"You don't have to beg... we'll take some of this food off your hands." Mo hurriedly sat down while his wife stood there shaking her head at him. "Come on baby, I'm going on the walk with you, right?"

Tara gave in and sat down on the blanket with them.

Then Mo said, "Now isn't this nice? You wanted to take a walk. But as a bonus I'm even taking you on a double date."

"What double date." Tara twisted her lip. "You didn't pay for any of this food. We are just two moochers interrupting a romantic picnic as far as I'm concerned."

Angel laughed but then she told Tara. "It's really not a problem, girl. Demetrius and I haven't been on a double date in a long time. So, this is fun."

"See," Mo poked at his wife. "Demetrius ballin' like a rock star so he can spare us some grub."

"I wish I was ballin' like a rock star," Demetrius said.

"You're a rock star to me," Angel told him. Then she said to Mo, "My man works hard for his money. He's a legit businessman who gets up every morning and goes to his office."

Mo tore into his piece of fried chicken like a pit bull taking a bite out of his prey. "What's this about legit? You don't work for your father anymore?"

Demetrius nodded. "But I handle our legitimate businesses. You remember the drive-thru Don bought all those years ago and the laundromat. I now manage a grocery store and a cleaners."

"And it's all legit?" Mo eyes widened as if he just couldn't believe what he was hearing.

Demetrius didn't look at Angel as he answered. "Yep, it's all legit. I'm not making money hand over fist like Don and his boys. So, the next time we do a double date… you can pay."

"Hey, I work for Frankie. He's the stingiest cat on the streets. So, I'm not making money like that either."

Demetrius had been enjoying his old friend's company. They'd seen each other in passing and said 'hey' and 'what's up', but they hadn't actually sat down and talked in years. After the way Don and Al had treated Mo, Demetrius understood his need to keep his distance. However, Demetrius had longed to rebuild their friendship and had thought about calling Mo up. But if Frankie's name was going to come out of his mouth every time they were together, then it might be best to just keep distance between them.

Mo and Tara finished their plate and then got up in order to take that nature walk. But before they walked away, Mo, turned back to Demetrius and said, "Let me holler at you."

Demetrius got up and he and Mo stepped away from the ladies. Then Mo said, "I've been wanting to give you a call for a few months now. Because I think you're about to run into some trouble with Frankie."

Demetrius tried to shut him down. "I don't have no dealings with Frankie. He deal directly with Don."

"I'm not talking about that. This is personal for Frankie." Mo stopped talking, checked his surroundings. "Look, I shouldn't even be saying anything to you… but you're my boy."

"Spill it already."

"You did remember that Frankie almost went pro back in the day, right?"

"Pro what?" Demetrius didn't know what Mo was getting at.

23

"Frankie played college football, man. He was going pro and everything until he busted out his knee. Anyway, he heard that DeMarcus is in football. And every since he's been spouting off about how the adoption wasn't legal. And about taking what's his."

"There is nothing in my house that belongs to Frankie Day. But I do wish he'd try to come get something... it'll be the last thing he does."

Three

The War Begins…

Don Shepherd called a meeting with his lieutenants. Stan Michaels, his best friend since they were in grade school together. Al Gamer the enforcer, who took care of issues with his fists or a bullet, and it didn't much matter which was used, the result was deadly. Joe-Joe Thornton was the third and final lieutenant. These men weren't just street business associates, they were like brothers; when one hurt, the other hurt also.

Demetrius sat in the back of the room wondering why his father had asked him to come to this meeting. Ever since the incident over ten years ago, when Al and the gang accused him of treason against his father, he was left out of the loop on anything the Four Musketeers thought of as sensitive or need-to-know information.

Al pointed in Demetrius' direction as he asked Don, "What's he doing here? I thought we were meeting about business tonight."

"We are, and it concerns Demetrius, since he handles all of the storefronts," Don told him.

"What?" Joe-Joe smirked as he asked, "Is the kid stealing from us now too?"

The group burst out in laughter.

They were never going to let him forget about the time he stopped them from killing an old friend of his. But Demetrius didn't care, they could laugh at him, and shun him all they wanted. All that mattered was that Coach Johnson and his wife, Katherine, were still alive and living good in South Carolina. He had beaten his father and his 'brothers' at their own game, and even though he hadn't turned on them in over a decade, they still couldn't find a way to forgive him.

Don put a hand on his son's shoulder. "Demetrius needs to be here. We've got a big problem, and I need us all on the lookout for what's coming next."

Don and his gang had started their criminal enterprise in the seventies with the street lottery and loan sharking. But they graduated to crack in the eighties. It was now the early nineties and Don Shepherd was sitting on top of a throne. He had the west and southwest region of Ohio on lock. Street dealers came to his comrades for their supplies, or they didn't do business in the state; it was as simple as that.

But there was a new hustler in town, who had brought with him a gang that wasn't interested in playing by the rules. They were trying to take over and Don wasn't having it. Michael Crane has become a problem."

"I told you that boy wasn't up to no good when he got here." Stan was up, angrily moving around the room. "Come telling me that he wanted to do business with us, but kept trying to find out where our shipment was coming in... then he asked me about our supplier."

"You should have put a bullet in him right then and there," Al said.

"Is killing folks the only solution you can come up with to handle a problem?" Demetrius asked Al.

"Is hiding folks and becoming a turn-coat the only solution you got to stop me?" Al fired back.

Don put a hand up, silencing the room. "We don't have time to argue amongst ourselves. The thing is, Michael Crane as made contact with our supplier and if we don't stop him, they are about to do business with the little insect.

Joe-Joe piped up. "How'd he find out who our supplier is?"

As Joe-Joe asked the question, Stan, Al and Joe-Joe started staring in Demetrius' direction. Demetrius got out of his seat. "I don't need this. I'm going home to my family."

"Don't leave yet son, there is a reason I asked you to join this meeting."

Demetrius had his hand on the door knob. He let it go and turned back to his father. Pointing at the others in the room, he said, "Then you need to check your boys. Because I'm not going to keep taking crap from them."

"Sit down Son, this is about business." As Demetrius took his seat, Don glanced around the room at the rest of them. "It's been ten years, fellas. Time to let it go. Don't you think?"

"Your son, your problem," Al said, then added, "I'll leave him be so we can get down to business."

Don fist bumped Al and then turned back to the group. "As I was saying, our supplier has guaranteed me that if we increase our shipment, then they'll make sure Crane and his crew get lost for good, if you get my drift."

"How much more?" Stan asked.

"A ton more." Don turned to Demetrius. "That's why you're here. We'll need to funnel money from our legit businesses in order to do this without the Feds figuring out what we're up to."

"Okay, but the businesses only make so much. I don't know how much you're trying to pull out, but I doubt we're earning enough to handle any real action." Angel had begged Demetrius to stay far away from his father's drug business. And for the most part he'd been able to do that. But from time to time, when his dad needed to move money around. There was nothing Demetrius could do. He had to get involved. And if he had to keep Angel in the dark about these transactions, then that was the way it had to be.

"I just bought a piece of land on Gettysburg. And I signed it over to you. I want you to relocate our businesses onto this land. You'll be dealing with contractors for the new buildings… we'll funnel the money to our supplier through them. But I'm going to need you to work with the contractors." Don told him. "Your name will be on all of our businesses, and you'll be signing all the contracts for the land and everything else. Got it?"

Demetrius leaned back and kicked up his feet. "Hey I'm paid very well for what I do. And now I'm actually going to own the business. I'm not complaining, believe that."

"Why should you," Don admonished. "You're a businessman. I finally did something for you that would make your mama proud, right?"

Demetrius' mama would probably prefer that the businesses weren't a front for drugs, but his mom was dead, so she didn't get a say. "Yeah Dad, she'd be proud."

"I almost forgot." Joe-Joe jumped out of his seat. "I ran into an old friend of yours, Don. She asked me to give you her number. But I left my cell phone in the car. I'll be right back."

"What's this woman's name?" Don asked.

"I don't remember. But the woman was fine, you hear me."

Don gave him a skeptical look. "Just go get me the number."

"You better hope he took a picture of her, because I saw what Joe-Joe considers fine. And she was a three-hundred pounder with finger waves in her head." Stan told the group.

"Hey, don't knock big women," Joe-Joe told them as he opened the front door. "I haven't gone hungry since I met her, cause the girl can burn."

Al was bent over laughing as he said, "I'd rather get take-out than to have some big 'ol woman rolling over on me while I'm trying to sleep."

The group was so busy laughing it up that none of them noticed the car parked in front of Don's house. But as the front door closed and Joe-Joe walked toward the drive-way the bullets started flying.

"Did y'all hear that?" Don jumped out of his seat, grabbed his gun and ran outside with Al, Stan and Demetrius on his heels.

As the gang burst through the front door they saw Joe-Joe laying on the ground and a car speeding off. Al and Don crouched down and started shooting.

Stan and Demetrius grabbed Joe-Joe's shoulders and pulled him towards the house.

"They got me," Joe-Joe said as blood pooled from his mouth.

"No," Stan yelled at Joe-Joe. "Don't you die on us. Not like this."

But Joe-Joe's body had already gone limp as he closed his eyes for the last time.

Demetrius hugged the man who had been more like an uncle to him. As he lifted himself from Joe-Joe's lifeless body, tears were streaming down his face.

Al was on his cell phone calling for an ambulance.

Don walked over to Demetrius and wiped the tears from his face. "Don't cry, Son. We're going to leave all the tears for those fools who thought they could get this off on us."

Stan, Al and Don bent down next to Joe-Joe. There was no pulse, no bringing him back and they all knew it. Anger burned deep, one of their brothers had been taken out.

Don looked to Stan and Al. Vengeance was in his eyes. "Y'all ready for this?"

Stan nodded.

Al said, "Ain't never stopped being ready."

"Good, cause there ain't gon' be no peace in this city. Not until we get justice for Joe-Joe."

Four

Joe-Joe was pronounced dead at 8:45 that evening. By ten o'clock, three crack houses had been sprayed with bullets. The next morning, Michael Crane's second in command, Lou Dawg was gunned down in front of the county court house as he tried to enter the building to pay his speeding ticket.

By that afternoon, Michael tried to call a truce with Don. Told him that he would personally kill every man, woman and child in his family if he didn't show himself within a week… so, no truce.

Demetrius decided that his family needed to get out of town for a while, at least until his father had handled his business. Angel was in the kitchen cooking dinner while KeKe watched. He said, "I thought KeKe was supposed to cook the dinners from now on?"

Angel smiled at KeKe as she told her husband, "I'm teaching her a few things."

"Well, you'll have to finish those lessons in Winston Salem, because I'm putting you and the kids on a flight to NC tonight."

Angel turned over the pieces of chicken she was frying, and then put her fork down. "What are you talking about, Demetrius? Don't you want us here for Joe-Joe's funeral?"

He shook his head. "You and the kids have got to go, Angel. I can't explain it now. Just trust that I know what I'm talking about."

Hands on hips, Angel twisted her lip. "Why are you staying, if we need to go so bad? What going on?"

KeKe very gently put a hand on Angel's shoulder as she said, "You need to listen to Demetrius, Angel. It's getting real on them streets and you need to get them kids out of harm's way."

"What has your father gotten you involved in now, Demetrius?" Angel searched her husband's face for answers, but she couldn't figure him out.

"Do you want me to pack for you?" Demetrius asked her.

"I'll go pack. But I want answers before I leave this house."

As Angel headed upstairs, KeKe turned to Demetrius. "It's bad isn't it?"

"You heard about what's going on?"

KeKe nodded. "Word is, your daddy's trying to make the whole city pay for what happened to Joe-Joe."

"Angel hasn't heard any of this, has she?"

KeKe shook her head. "Angel didn't grow up here, so she don't really have any friends other than you and me. And I sure wasn't going to tell her about this."

"Good." Demetrius patted her on the shoulder. "Good."

When Angel came back down the stairs she told Demetrius that she had packed the bags for the kids and asked him to go upstairs and get them. Once he had left the kitchen, she turned to KeKe. "I don't want you to stay in this house while I'm gone."

KeKe's eyes widened. "You don't have to worry about me, Angel. Demetrius is like a brother to me. I would never do you like that."

Shaking her head, Angel waved that notion away. "I wasn't implying that you would try to get with Demetrius while I'm gone. I just know my husband, and if he wants me out of town so quickly, then his dad is up to something. And I don't want you to get hurt because you became a convenient target for one of Don Shepherd's enemies."

"But you know my situation, Angel. My family has drug problems. Then I could be looking at another setback. And then I'll never get my kids."

"I want you to come with me. My parents are great people and they would love to host all of us."

"I've got the bags," Demetrius told them as he entered the room. "Let's pick up the kids from school and head to the airport."

"How about it, KeKe? You're more than welcome to stay in our home while I'm gone, but I really think you'll be safer with us than you will be in this house."

A smile crept across KeKe's face as she wrapped her arms around Angel and hugged her. "I have never had anyone look after me the way you two have. I wish I really was your sister."

After seeing his family off, Demetrius then prepared himself to meet up with the last person he wanted to see on God's green earth. Since his daddy was busy avenging Joe-Joe's death and making arrangements for the funeral, Demetrius had to pick up the slack on a few distribution deals.

Frankie Day used to be a small time strip club owner who was also a part-time pimp. About five years ago, he'd come up in the world when he put together enough money to become one of the top drug dealers on the street. He bought all of his product from Don, so even though Demetrius wanted nothing to do with the man, his father and Frankie had become friendly. According to Don, even while burying one of his best friends, Frankie's call needed to be honored.

So, even though Demetrius handled the business side of the operation, today he was forced to deal with slime like Frankie.

"Demetrius, my man," Frankie said, and they slapped hands. "Thanks for bringing this special delivery all the way over here."

"Don't thank me. Don says that whatever you want... whenever you want it, it's a done deal."

Frankie nodded. "Don has been good to me through the years... all except for that time he sent you to break my legs." Frankie tried to laugh, but Demetrius knew the events of that night behind Frankie's strip club, still didn't sit right with the man.

"All's well that ends well, ain't that right?" Frankie said, trying to lighten the mood.

"If you say, so Frankie."

Frankie stepped back, gave Demetrius a look that made it clear where they stood... he despised him. "I would think you would say that it ended well, Demetrius. I mean, you did walk out of here with not only my baby's mama, but with my son as well. By the way, how is *my* son?"

Angel had used extremely poor judgement in picking the men in her life, before she and Demetrius got together. Frankie had tried to use and abuse her, even though she should have been at home taking care of his kid. DeMarcus had been two years old when he came to live in Demetrius's house. The boy had been calling him daddy since that age. DeMarcus was now thirteen and Demetrius would kill Frankie before he allowed him to lay claim to *his* son. "Your goods are in the back of my truck. Do you have some guys to help unload?"

"Of course I've got some guys." Frankie called his boys out and had them unload the stuff. While he and Demetrius stood watching, he couldn't resist one last dig. "DeMarcus plays football with one of my other sons. I saw his last game. The boy is NFL bound. Just like his daddy." Frankie then touched his knee. "If I hadn't blown out my knee, I would have gotten that call on draft day for sure."

Why his father felt the need to do business with Frankie, was beyond Demetrius' understanding. But this was his last delivery to this man. He got behind the wheel and closed his door.

Just as Demetrius was about to pull off, Frankie hollered at him. "Tell Angel it was real nice seeing her the other day."

"Don't let my wife's name fall out your mouth again, or it will be the last time." As Demetrius drove off all he heard was roaring laughter coming from Frankie. Like he knew something Demetrius didn't. He pulled his car into the Save-A-Lot parking lot and pulled out his cell phone. Angel's plane would be landing in about twenty minutes. He had work to do, but he would call Angel later, because she had some explaining to do.

Five

Maxine Barnes opened her front door to find Angel, her three grandsons and another woman standing on her porch. Her hand immediately went to her mouth as her eyes widened with joy. She reached out and hugged every one of them, and then ushered them in to the house. "Now Angel, why didn't you tell me y'all were coming. I could have prepared the house for you... Is Demetrius coming too?"

Shaking her head, Angel told her, "It's just us this trip." Then she pointed to KeKe. "I want to introduce you to KeKe. She's been helping me with the house and the kids for about a month now."

"Didn't I speak to you when I called for Angel last week?" Maxine asked.

"Yes, ma'am." KeKe extended her hand and they shook.

"Lucky for y'all, I had just put on a big pot of chicken noodle soup. Or y'all would just have to settle for eating a pizza."

In unison, the kids started jumping around. "Pizza... pizza... pizza."

"Now you've gotten them started, Mama." Angel shook her head.

Maxine was all smiles. "DeMarcus, go into my bedroom and get my purse. I think I just might order that pizza for you boys after all."

"They can eat chicken noodle soup with the rest of us and they'll like it," Angel said, with a look of warning.

But Dee got down on his knees and begged his grandmother to give them pizza.

KeKe started laughing. She then asked Angel for the key to the rental car. "I'll go get our bags."

"That's a good idea, and these boys can help you." Maxine said as she picked up the telephone and ordered a large pepperoni.

Angel just shook her head. "You never would have let me and Ronny get away with that."

"Grandmothers have certain privileges. Especially when they don't get to see their grandchildren all the time." Maxine grabbed her daughter's hand and walked her into the family room. "Now sit down with me and tell me what's going on."

Angel didn't like lying to her mother, which was one of the reasons that she'd lobbied so hard for Demetrius to take over the business side of Don's operation. She didn't like having to explain gangster stuff to her parents, but here she was being run out of town because of something her father-in-law had going on.

"All I know is one of my father-in-law's friends got shot and killed a couple of days ago. And I guess whatever is going on has Demetrius worried that something might happen to us if we stay at the house."

Maxine lowered her head and started praying. "My Lord, my Lord. Help, Lord Jesus, Help!"

"It's no big deal, Mama. Demetrius is just being overly cautious because he doesn't want anything to happen to us."

"That's one good thing," Maxine said, and then added, "But if he's all that concerned, you'd think he'd stop all of this dirty dealing with that father of his."

"It's not even like that, Mama. Demetrius runs businesses for his father. We have a drive-thru, a laundromat, cleaners, and small grocery store. I've even helped out when he needed me. I don't know what I have to do to convince you that everything is on the up and up with those businesses."

"If you say that Demetrius is doing the right thing, then that's good enough for me." Maxine stood up. "Let me call your dad and let him know that you and the boys are here."

As Maxine left the room Angel's cell phone rang. She opened her purse and pulled her phone out. It was Demetrius. "Hey baby, you have such good timing. We just made it to my parent's house."

"How was your flight?" he asked.

The words he spoke were normal, but her husband didn't sound normal. "Is everything alright up there? Did something happen after I left?"

"As a matter of fact, something did happen... I ran into Frankie."

Before she could stop herself, Angel gasped.

"So he was telling the truth. He has seen you. Did you let him see DeMarcus?"

"Did he come into one of the stores just to tell you he ran into me? What a loser." Angel detested Frankie Day, and wished that she had never met him in the first place. But when she started thinking like that, she reminded herself how wonderful her son is, and then she just tried to put Frankie out of her thoughts all together. DeMarcus didn't remember anything about the man, and she intended to keep it that way.

"It doesn't matter where I ran into him, the fact is that you never said a word to me about seeing Frankie. Why would you hide something like that from me?"

Angel didn't understand why Demetrius was getting so worked up about this. She totally trusted her husband. Because in the ten years they have been married, he hadn't given her one reason to doubt him. She thought that Demetrius felt the same about her. "Why you coming at me like this? I saw him at one of DeMarcus' football games. You had to work at the grocery store that morning so you couldn't make the game."

"Since I wasn't there that sucka felt like he could rush up on you, is that what happened?" Demetrius asked.

"I don't know about rushing up on me... but me and the kids were walking toward the field so I could get DeMarcus and go home. He bumped into me, said excuse me. Then he made some lame comment about DeMarcus being able to go pro if he stayed healthy."

"And what did you say?" Demetrius demanded.

"I didn't say anything. I probably glared at him for a second and then I walked away from him. That's it. End of story."

"Do you think DeMarcus saw him?"

Angel's mom came back into the room. Angel told her that she needed to finish her call and then went out to the back patio. When DeMarcus was a baby he looked more like Angel, but in the past five years as he stretched and grew, more and more of Frankie's features started cropping up. Demetrius had mentioned DeMarcus' changing features to her on two separate occasions, but Angel didn't think it was a big deal.

Now she was wondering if this was going to be a problem. "Demetrius, you have to be reasonable. We don't live in some huge city, so we are going to run into Frankie from time to time."

Demetrius grunted. "I know that, Angel. I guess," he hesitated. "I just don't want... DeMarcus is my son, and I don't want some other man laying claim to him."

Angel loved Demetrius with all of her heart. He might be the son of a gangster, but Demetrius had a good heart and he was her man, now and forever. She didn't want him feeling insecure about where he stood with DeMarcus; but, from time to time, she did wonder if they had done a disservice to DeMarcus by not telling him the truth. "Demetrius, I know you're not going to like this, but do you think that we should sit DeMarcus down and tell him that Frankie is his father."

"No!" Demetrius exploded.

But Angel barely heard the thunderous sound of her husband's voice, because at that moment her eyes shifted toward DeMarcus. He'd been hiding on the side of the porch, but had popped his head up and was now staring at her with tears in his eyes. "Oh my God," Angel screamed. "DeMarcus, baby, come here."

"DeMarcus is outside? Why didn't you tell me that?" Demetrius asked.

"Who is Frankie, Mama?" DeMarcus asked as he came closer to her.

"Nobody, baby. Nobody at all." She put the cell phone on speaker and handed it to DeMarcus. "Here, talk to your daddy. I need to sit down for a minute."

DeMarcus was crying as he talked to Demetrius. "Daddy?"

"Yeah, son, I'm here."

"Are you my daddy?"

"Of course I'm your daddy. Haven't I been here all of your life? Think back DeMarcus. Has there ever been anyone else in your life but me and your mama?"

"No," he answered while wiping his face. "But I heard mama say."

"Don't you worry about what your mama said. I was saying something to her that I never should have brought up. I'm sorry, DeMarcus. Your mama and I never should have been talking like that. But you are my son. Do you hear me?"

"I hear you, Daddy."

"Hand the phone back to your mama and then I want you to go back in the house and check on your brothers."

"Okay Daddy."

"I think we just broke our son's heart, Demetrius," Angel said after DeMarcus had gone inside and closed the door.

"I'm so sorry, Angel. I should have waited until you got home. But Frankie got me all riled up... I wanted to break his legs and then stuff his foot down his throat."

"Just stay away from him." She stood up, preparing to go inside and face her son again. "And you better be figuring out what we are going to do about DeMarcus. Because I can guarantee you that we haven't heard the last of this."

"I'll make it right, Angel. I promise you that. If it's the last thing I do on earth. I'll make this right for DeMarcus."

She wanted to be angry at Demetrius. His stupid jealousy had just ruined everything that they had spent years building. DeMarcus would probably never trust them again... not once he discovered the truth that they had kept from him all these years. But as she thought back to that fateful day when Demetrius had agreed to be DeMarcus's daddy, Angel knew that the deceit had started as they

41

traveled Winston-Salem, NC to see her parents. Angel had been so ashamed of coming back home as an unwed mother, and of the thought of having to tell her parents that DeMarcus' father owned a strip club; that she'd turned to Demetrius for help. She still remembered everything about that night. How they had been on the run from his father... how they had tried to save his baseball coach's life... the night Demetrius betrayed his father and showed her that he was the kind of man she could love for a life time.

"Angel came into his life at the right time. And now that he has a son, it's time for Demetrius to realize that he needs to change his life," Katherine was saying as they sat in Demetrius' SUV waiting on him to pull up so they could get on the highway and whisk Coach Johnson and his wife, Katherine away to safety.

Angel gave a half smile as she said, "Maybe... I hope so." She couldn't bring herself to admit that DeMarcus wasn't Demetrius' son. She didn't want this couple, who loved so deeply to know what a fool she had been. And as they kept sitting there, waiting on Demetrius, she realized that her mother would want to know about DeMarcus's father. How could she tell her that she'd left home to shack up with a strip club owner, who dealt drugs to his customers and tried to pimp her out. How could she tell her sweet mother that DeMarcus's father was a heartless man like that?

Just as the shame of the situation was about to overtake her and cause her to rethink this visit with her mother, DeMarcus got fidgety in his seat, as he pointed at something outside and said, "Daddy."

Angel's head swiveled around, 'please God,' she silently prayed. 'Let it be Demetrius'. A silver SUV had just parked next to them. As Angel glanced over with panic in her eyes, she saw that Demetrius was in the driver's seat. Once again he had proven that she could trust him. He hadn't hopped on that plane and left her behind. He got out and then Angel got out and ran to him. She jumped into his arms and sprinkled kisses all over his face.

Laughing, he asked, "What's all of this for?"

"Demetrius Shepherd, you are a man of your word and I love you for that."

They took all of the bags out of his SUV and put them in the one he had rented. Angel was confused as to why this had to be done, so she asked, "If I'm going to follow you, why do we need to take our stuff out of your SUV?"

"You and DeMarcus will ride with us. I'm going to leave my SUV here."

"But if you leave it here, somebody might steal it or something," Angel said.

"And if we take it, my father might be able to find us that much faster." He opened the door for her. "Let's go."

Once the women and the baby were in the car, Coach Johnson caught Demetrius by the shoulder and said, "I'm sorry for the way I treated you the other day. I shouldn't have assumed that you knew what your father was up to."

"I'm glad you spoke up," Demetrius told him, and then added, "Look, the real truth is, I don't know if my father is sending someone after you tonight. But if he is, I couldn't live with myself if I just let you die."

"Don isn't going to like this," Coach warned.

That was the understatement of the century, but Demetrius wasn't going to dwell on it. "You told me that you wanted to move south, do you know where you want to go?"

"Columbia, South Carolina," Coach said without giving it a second thought. My son lives there. And with all that's happened, it would do my wife some good to be around the boy and that new grand baby of ours."

"Okay, so we'll drop you there, then I'm taking Angel to Winston-Salem, North Carolina to see her people. I think we'll stay in the South for a week or two. Give my father a little time to cool off."

"What if he pressures you for my location? I don't want anything to happen to my family."

Demetrius put an arm on Coach Johnson's shoulder. "You were good to me when I was a kid. I'll never forget you, Coach... and I'd never tell my father anything about your son. So, don't worry. He won't find you."

They took the back roads out of Ohio into West Virginia. By the time they reached Virginia they were dead tired, so they checked into a hotel. Once Angel, Demetrius and DeMarcus were alone in their room and getting ready for bed, she told him, "I need to talk to you."

Demetrius was carrying DeMarcus on his back. He put him down. "What's up?"

She sat down next to DeMarcus and she said, "I'm kind of embarrassed about this. But Katherine assumed that Mar-Mar is your son, and I didn't correct her."

Demetrius gave her a look that said 'who cares'.

"The thing is, I need a favor from you. And I know that I have no right to ask this, especially since I didn't want you to have anything to do with DeMarcus when we first came to your house."

"Just tell me what you need, Angel. After what you did for me today, I'll move heaven and earth to make you happy."

She smiled at him. He was becoming her hero; she just didn't want to overstep her boundaries and mess up everything. But yet and still, she had to ask. "I told you that I come from a broken home because my father cheated on my mother. But what I didn't tell you is that my father is a preacher."

"He's what? I thought you said the guy was no good?"

"He's not." Angel's mouth tightened as she said, "But that doesn't matter. What does matter, is that despite what my father did, my family is super conservative. It would break my mother's heart to know who DeMarcus's father is."

Lowering her head in shame, she added, "I don't want them to know anything that I've been through, so I'm asking that you pretend that DeMarcus is your son and that we are in love."

He lifted her head with his index finger. When she was looking him in the eye, he said, "We are in love... and DeMarcus already calls me daddy, so I doubt it would be hard to convince them of that."

"So you'll do it?"

He nodded.

Angel wrapped her arms around him. "You are too good to me. Thank you so much."

Angel had thought she'd come up with the best way to cover her shame, but had she destroyed her son in the process? Would the lies she had told all these years cause her son to hate her?

Six

DeMarcus was heartbroken and Demetrius had to fix it. He was so angry with himself for allowing Frankie's taunts to cause him to become so enraged that he got into an argument with his wife, now their secret was unraveling. Demetrius knew that Frankie meant nothing to Angel. So, as he sat next to his father in the front row of the funeral home, he lowered his head as tears threatened to roll down his face.

Don put a hand on his shoulder and whispered, "We can get through this. Joe-Joe wouldn't want us crying."

Demetrius looked at his father, he was about to tell him that he wasn't emotional over Joe-Joe today. But about his son, but that's when he noticed that his father's eyes were red. Don might not be crying now, but he had shed some tears over Joe-Joe's death. He squeezed his father's hand. "We can do this."

When the funeral was over, Al, Stan, Don and Demetrius carried Joe-Joe's gold plated casket to the awaiting hearse. They drove over to Woodland Cemetery, and then the boys took Joe-Joe's casket to its final resting place. The funeral home had been filled to capacity, and as they stood around the gravesite, Demetrius was thankful that so many people had paid their respects.

After the preacher said a few words and many of the people who'd gathered to say goodbye to a fallen gangster threw pink, yellow and red roses in the ground where Joe-Joe's body would be placed, they headed back to their cars. The boys stayed planted, choosing to spend one last moment with their friend… their brother.

The funeral director had already been instructed to re-open the casket once the crowd had left, so he did as he was told and then left them alone.

"Well Joe-Joe, I guess this is it," Al said as he placed a rose in the casket. Al, then turned his back, not wanting to look at his old friend like that for any longer than he had too.

"It was real nice knowing you, Unc." Demetrius put a rose in the casket as well, and then moved out of the way.

Stan started laughing, but it was a sorrowful kind of laugh. He nudged Don as he said, "Remember when this little scrawny kid approached us, talking 'bout he wanted to skip school too."

Don smiled. "It was tenth grade wasn't it? And we were trying to shoot craps rather than attend our science class."

"Yeah, Joe-Joe was a freshman, and we told him to go back to class and leave grown men alone."

Don added, "That's when he showed us the stack of cash he had, and we took him to that crap game and won all his dough."

"That boy was such a sucker," Stan said.

Don nodded in agreement. "But he had heart. So, we watched out for him, and stopped anybody else from getting an advantage on him." Don sniffed, and as he turned to Stan, tears crept down his face. "We got to finish this, Stan. We let somebody get an advantage on Joe-Joe, and we swore we would never do that."

"It's as good as done, Don. And you can take that to the bank, my friend." Stan then placed his rose in Joe-Joe's casket and walked away.

Don wiped the tear from his face, put it on one of the rose pedals and then placed it in the coffin with his friend. He then closed the coffin lid. As Don and the gang then headed toward their cars they had no words for each other. But words weren't needed.

The song, "It's So Hard to Say Goodbye to Yesterday" played in Demetrius' head. But he wasn't just thinking about Joe-Joe. His son was on his mind also. Because Demetrius had a feeling that things would never be the same between them, and he had nobody but himself to blame.

"Get down!" Don yelled and then dived on Demetrius.

Stan and Al took out their guns and started shooting.

Don asked Demetrius, "Did you get hit?"

Demetrius patted his chest and his arms. "I don't feel anything. They must have missed me." Sitting up, Demetrius looked around. "Where did they come from? I didn't see or hear that car. The only thing I felt was the wind blowing around me."

"Boy, your head was down. I taught you to always keep your eyes open. I thought for sure you got hit. Those bullets were coming straight at you."

~~~~~

Saul hadn't been called to duty on Demetrius or Angel's behalf in about a decade. But as the heavens opened, Saul was standing next to his captain viewing Demetrius and the gang of thugs he called a family as they walked away from a gravesite toward their cars. Demetrius's head was low, he had so much on his mind that he wasn't paying attention to what was going on. A car was pulling into the graveyard.

Captain Aaron pointed toward the car. "The gunmen in this car are about to kill Demetrius."

Saul's eyes widened. "But his father is there, why wouldn't they kill him? Isn't he the one causing all the trouble?"

"You are correct, Don Shepherd is a bad man. But Demetrius is broken hearted right now. He's not able to defend himself from this attack as the other men are. You will have to go and help him because the child has yet to be born, and Demetrius must take part in his upbringing."

Saul saluted his captain, then unsheathed his sword and went into action. As the car pulled up closer to the gang, the windows rolled down and gunmen leaned out of the car and started shooting.

With his sword lifted, Saul circled around Demetrius, creating a force field of protection, so the bullet that was meant to hit Demetrius' heart and kill him instantly simply fell to the ground. When Saul saw Don Shepherd running toward his son, he released the force of protection and the two men fell to the ground.

~~~~

"What has got you so out of sorts today?" Don asked as he and Demetrius drove down the street.

Rubbing his temples, Demetrius let out his frustration by hitting the side of the door. "I messed up."

They came to a red light, Don turned to his son. "Don't tell me, my son, the choir boy actually cheating on his wife?"

"No, why would you think something like that?"

"Angel left town, didn't she?"

Demetrius eyed his father as if he was going senile. "Of course she left town. You've got the vendetta going on and I didn't want my family to get hurt in the crossfires."

"I take care of what's mine, believe that," Don said as he pulled into his driveway.

"Why are we here? I thought you were driving me home?"

"Nah, things are a little too hot for you to go to that house all by your lonesome. You're going to stay with me and Lisa for a few days… or at least long enough for me to figure out what's got you out of sorts."

"It's nothing to do with the business, Dad." Demetrius hesitated a moment, then said, "DeMarcus overheard me and his mom arguing about Frankie, and now he knows that I'm not his biological father."

"And?" Don's cell phone rang as he and Demetrius got out of the car and headed inside. "Hold that thought. Let me get this."

Demetrius plopped down on the snow white sofa in the sitting room. The liquor cabinet was in this room, and he was trying to decide if he wanted a drink as his father was saying…

"That's good Al, I didn't even think about taking a picture of the license plate… did you give that info to one of our boys down at the police station? Okay, when he gets that name to you hit me back."

Don hung up the phone and Demetrius asked, "Al found out who shot at us?"

"He's having one of our guys at the police station run the plates. We'll know soon enough." Don held up a hand, but let's get back to your problem." He shrugged a shoulder, "What's the big deal? So the kid knows that you're not the biological father. DeMarcus is still our family and we'd never treat him any different."

"I just don't know what to do, dad. My son is confused and heartbroken over this. I don't know how to fix it, because I'm not about to share custody with the likes of Frankie Day."

"See this is why I don't like secrets," Don said as he closed the garage door behind them. "You know how my sweet mother, God rest her soul, found out who her real father was?"

"How?"

"At a family reunion. She told me that a woman ran to her and gave her a hug. She then told her, 'I'm your Aunt Betty'."

Demetrius's brow lifted. "But Grandpa Dave didn't have any sisters."

"Tell me about it," Don said. "My mom was thirty-seven and I was seventeen when we found out that her real dad was a man named Otis. And wouldn't you know it, good ol' Otis was already dead. So, there was no reason to spill the beans."

"Otis, who?" Lisa asked as she walked into the room holding a glass in her hand. It was two in the afternoon and she still had on this long flowing night gown that showed more cleavage than her stepson should be able to see.

"You don't know him," Don said with a distasteful look on his face.

Lisa set her glass on the bar as she opened the liquor cabinet.

"Getting started already, dear?" Don asked.

Lisa laughed as she put a few ice cubes in her glass and then poured bourbon. "I started when I woke up, dear," She returned the endearment, but 'Dear' sounded like a bad thing when she said it. "This is my third drink. Would you like to join me? How about you, Demetrius?"

Demetrius shook his head.

Don said, "No, I don't want a drink, what I'd like is for you to get to the Betty Ford clinic and dry out. I didn't marry you so I could watch a lush ruin her kidneys and die of cirrhosis of the liver."

"Thanks dear," she sneered the word 'deer' again. "Hopefully my clothes fit your girlfriend, so that when I'm dead, you can not only present her with this fabulous house, but a full wardrobe as well." Lisa took a big gulp of her drink, and then just as quietly as she entered the room, she left again.

Demetrius waited until he heard Lisa walking up the stairs, he leaned forward. "Dang Dad, I didn't know it had gotten that bad. When did Lisa start drinking so much?"

"She claims that all my cheating has driven her to the bottle." Don twisted his lip as if he didn't believe that one, and then said, "Yeah, right."

"Why don't you stop cheating and see if she stops drinking?"

"Boy, you talking crazy. The ladies love your old man. I can't deprive them of all of this." Don stood up and flexed his muscles. Then his cell phone rang.

He answered it and said, "You got it... Come swoop me, I'm rolling with you."

Demetrius knew what that meant. Somebody was about to die tonight. He didn't have the stomach to deal with what he knew was about to happen, so he headed upstairs to the guest room, and took a nap. When he woke up, he picked up the remote and started changing channels.

An episode of the Cosby Show was playing, but Demetrius didn't want to watch some make-believe family, living some perfect, make-believe-life, so he kept flipping channels until he came to an episode of Law & Order. That was more his speed. Thugs against the justice system. Was there going to be order in the court today, or would the murderer go free?

Seven

Angel was sitting in the kitchen drinking a cup of iced coffee when her father, Pastor Marvin R. Barnes walked in. "I think we need to talk," he told her.

When Angel was a little girl, her father had been her hero. Angel had even dreamed of becoming a preacher just like her daddy. But then her daddy had an affair and it tore their family apart. Angel spent many years, hating him for what he had done.

At the age of sixteen, Angel ran away from home because she didn't think anything would ever be right again with her dad no longer in the house with them. She'd spent some hard years living on her own and received the hard knocks of life, but then Demetrius came into her life. He was the one who made it possible for Angel to come back home. That's when she discovered that her parents were back together. But she also discovered that her mother had a stroke. The stroke happened within a few weeks of Angel's disappearance.

Angel didn't understand how her mother could have forgiven her father for what he'd done to their family. But as the years passed and she began to recognize that even though her mother had been weakened by her father's affair and the subsequent divorce, Maxine Barnes had still been left standing... until her daughter ran away, and then within three weeks after Angel's foolish actions, her mother had the stroke.

But not once in all the years that passed had Maxine ever blamed Angel for the fact that she would always have to depend on a cane, because her left leg was still weak from the stroke. Angel saw that as her mother extending grace and forgiveness to her. The kind that she didn't even have to ask for.

Within the space of a few years, Angel had gone from not wanting her father at her wedding, to receiving him with open arms when he and Maxine came to the hospital the day she'd given birth to Dee.

Her father had just returned from the fishing trip he'd taken the boys on at five this morning. By the look on his face, she knew the conversation wasn't going to be good. "Did the boys catch any fish?" she asked, trying to lighten the mood.

"Of course they did. You know Papa taught them a little somethin' somethin'."

"Good. I'm glad y'all enjoyed the trip."

Pastor Marvin pulled up a chair and sat down at the table across from his daughter. He was silent for a moment as he bowed his head in prayer. When he raised his head, and looked at Angel once again, he told her, "I'm not trying to pry in your business. And I certainly am not judging you. What was done in the past is history as far as I'm concerned." But then he added, "But DeMarcus is hurting right now."

"I know he is, Daddy. But I don't know what to do. Demetrius tried to tell him to ignore what he heard, because he is and will always be his daddy. But DeMarcus won't let it go."

Sighing, Pastor Marvin said, "Do you remember when you let the boys spend the summer with us two years ago?"

Angel nodded. "The boys loved being down here. They want to come back again this summer. But first they want me and Demetrius to take them to Disney World." She almost chuckled, but she was too busy bracing herself for what was about to come.

"They did have fun," Marvin agreed. "But one thing that stands out for me now, was the day DeMarcus asked me why he didn't look like his brothers."

"He asked you that?" Angel was floored. She had never once imagined that DeMarcus was thinking like that.

"He did... I told him that a few years back he looked just like you and Ronny when y'all were kids, but that he must be coming into his own look. At the time, I had no reason to doubt that was the truth. But DeMarcus says he heard you explicitly say that his father is some guy by the name of Frankie."

Angel shut her eyes, trying to block out the fact that her greatest lie was now being exposed. What was she supposed to do about the mess that she had created? As she reopened her eyes, her father was still looking at her, waiting on a response. She could just tell her father to stay out of their business and then storm out of the room. But she couldn't do that to him. It was time for her to fess up.

"The truth is that DeMarcus' father didn't want anything to do with him after I gave birth. And after Demetrius and I fell in love and he brought me home to see you and mama, I was too ashamed to admit that I was an unwed mother with no husband in sight. So, I asked Demetrius to pretend to be DeMarcus' father... He officially adopted him after we got married, and we've been pretending every since."

"I'm sorry that we deceived you. But I was just too ashamed to tell the truth back then."

Pastor Marvin shook his head. "You don't owe me an apology. I know all about shame and how it can drive you to do the wrong thing for the right reason." He pulled his daughter close and hugged her. "Just take care of DeMarcus because you don't want to lose him the way I lost you."

"You're right Daddy. Demetrius and I will talk to DeMarcus."

~~~~

While Angel's father was giving her good advice to help hold her family together, Don Shepherd was busy trying to keep the family business intact the only way he knew how. He and Al had surprised the drive-by-shooter who had been dumb enough to use his own vehicle, and go back home with his buddies to smoke weed and laugh it up.

But they weren't laughing now, because Don and Al had the three bumbling idiots tied up as they tortured and grilled them for information. Al was using a pair of pliers to twist off the pinky finger of the guy who drove the car. "What? What'd you say? Speak up?"

"I said I'll tell you what you want to know."

Al put the pliers down and turned to Don. "Did you hear that? The man said he's ready to talk."

"Keep your mouth shut, Drake. You talk to them and we're dead," the guy tied up next to Drake said.

"You're dead already," Don told the guy and then put a bullet in him.

The man slumped over the third guy, who immediately started screaming. "Michael Crane sent us after you. He wants you dead real bad."

"Where is he?" The tone of Don's voice made it very clear that they had better have an answer.

Guy number three opened his mouth again. "He told us to meet him in front of the Kinko's downtown later on tonight so we could get paid."

Since the driver of the drive-by car hadn't offered up any information, Don turned his gun toward him and pulled the trigger. He then told Al to bring the snitch with them.

Al unhooked the boy from his now dead friends and then wrapped the rope back around his arms. As they headed out of the house, Al told him, "I hope you aren't lying. Because if you are, we aren't going to be as kind to you as we were to your friends... you will die slowly."

~~~~

"DeMarcus is moping around, refusing to talk to anybody but my daddy. And I really wish he hadn't said anything to daddy, but the secret is out now."

"I know," Demetrius agreed. "I've been sick about the whole thing myself." He thought about how he almost got shot earlier in the day, because he had his mind on DeMarcus rather than watching out for himself.

"I wish you were here with us. I worry about you, being left in that city when Don is on the war path about something."

"There's nothing to worry about. I'm staying at Dad's place tonight. Nothing's going on over here, matter of fact, I'm already in bed, just watching reruns on TV."

"How was the funeral?"

"It was good... a lot of people came out to pay their respects." He wasn't going to tell her about the ones who showed up to do a drive-by. "Daddy, laid Joe-Joe out like a king. You would have liked the service."

"I'm sorry that I had to miss it. I really liked Joe-Joe."

"I know you wanted to come to the funeral, but I just didn't think it would be safe. Turns out, there was nothing to worry about."

"Good," Angel said, "Then we should be able to come back home, right?"

"Yeah baby, just give it another day or two. Things should be calming down around here real soon."

"Okay, but what are we going to do about DeMarcus? According to my father, he had already been wondering why he didn't look like the rest of our kids. He even asked him about it two years ago."

"Wow, I never knew he even recognized a difference between him and his brothers."

"He does, Demetrius. And after overhearing me, he now knows for sure that you're not his father."

"I am his father!" Demetrius exploded. "I've been there since he was a baby. I wiped his nose, I fed him and put a roof over his head all these years. Not Frankie Day."

"I know that, Demetrius. But DeMarcus needs answers."

"I'm not sharing visitation rights with the likes of Frankie Day."

"Well, I don't know what you want me to do then, Demetrius. Because once we tell him the truth, he's going to want to see the man."

Demetrius shook his head. "That's never going to happen. DeMarcus is my son and as far as I'm concerned Frankie is nothing."

When Angel didn't respond, he said, "Do you agree with me or not?"

"Of course I agree with you. I know better than anyone that Frankie is nothing but scum. But we created this mess, and we've got to solve it."

Stretching out on the bed, Demetrius put his arm behind his head and laid there for a moment thinking. As the silence continued to fill the air, Demetrius remembered something his father had said. His grandmother had been told that the man she thought was her father, was actually not. But at the same time she'd also been told the man who was her father was dead. So, he said, "I'm more comfortable with a half-truth in this situation."

"What do you mean?" Angel asked.

"I'll agree to telling DeMarcus that Frankie is his biological father, as long as we also tell DeMarcus that Frankie is dead."

"What? We can't do that."

But Demetrius wasn't going to be denied. "When you came to me before we got married and asked me to pretend to be DeMarcus' father, I did you one better by adopting him and becoming his father for real. Now, I'm asking you to do this for me, because I can't share my son with another man, I just can't do it."

Before Angel could answer him, Don burst into his room. "Get downstairs, now," he said and then closed the door back.

Eight

Demetrius hung up with his wife and got downstairs on the double. He didn't know what his daddy was up to, but he was definitely up to something. Demetrius recognized that taking-care-of-business kind of look in his father's eye.

"What's going on?" Demetrius asked as he entered the kitchen. But one second after he asked the question, Demetrius saw Al pointing a gun at some guy who was seated at the kitchen table with his hands tied behind his back.

"Meet Russ Parker, one of the thugs who tried to kill you this afternoon," Al told him.

"What are you doing? Why did you bring him to the house?"

"We need you to keep an eye on Mr. Russ while we go find Michael Crane," Don said.

Demetrius wanted no parts of this. "Why me? Why didn't you just take him with you?"

"Boy, why don't you shut up and earn your keep around here," Al told him as he shoved the gun in his hand.

Demetrius knew that his father's boys didn't like the fact that he was paid a quarter of a million a year for running all of the legit businesses. They thought that to get money like that, he should have to get his hands dirty, whether he was Don's son or not. For the most part, Demetrius ignored their antagonistic remarks because he wasn't about to offer to do any more than he was already doing. He'd made his bones by breaking legs early on in his father's business. But Demetrius wasn't about that life, not now that he had a family to raise. So, he tried to reason with his father by saying, "What if Lisa wakes up and finds this guy tied up in her kitchen?"

Don laughed at that. "Are you kidding? Boy, that drunk is out for the night. You just hold it down here and wait for my call."

The gun was in Demetrius' right hand as he sat down across Russ. The guy was sweating, looking like he expected a bullet to be coming his way any minute. "Where's the rest of your crew? Wasn't it about three or four of y'all in that car?"

Russ' voice quivered as he said, "Your father shot them."

Demetrius should have figured that. And the fact that Russ' comment didn't even cause him to flinch should have told Demetrius how desensitized he'd become to all the violence around him. "What did you think was going to happen after y'all tried to take us out?"

"I didn't know where we were going. My cousin told me to hop in the car so we could go make some money... I lost my job last week and I've got two kids to feed. So, I rode with them."

"You didn't know what was going on?"

Tears rolled down Russ' face. "I made a bad decision and now I'm as good as dead... just trying to feed my family. Can't you understand that?"

"I really wish I could feel for you," Demetrius said as he got up and went to the refrigerator. "But if one of y'all had put a bullet in me, then I wouldn't be around to feed my family, now would I?" Demetrius pulled the turkey, ham and cheese out of the refrigerator and started making a sandwich.

After making his sandwich, Demetrius popped a can of soda and sat back down. He ate his sandwich in front of Russ without offering him anything. When Demetrius was finished with his food, he lifted Russ out of his seat by the collar of his shirt. "I'm not sitting in the kitchen all night with you."

They went to the family room, Demetrius shoved Russ into a seat. He then picked up the remote, turned on the television and started channel surfing. He kicked his feet up as he relaxed on the couch. His cell phone rang, Demetrius showed Russ his gun before answering, daring the man to say a word while he took the call.

"Hey baby, I'm sorry I didn't call you back."

"What did you father want?" Angel asked.

"He was just bugging me about work stuff… but he left the house again."

"So, what are you doing now?"

"Just channel surfing."

"I'm not going to keep you," she told him. "I just called back to tell you that I'm willing to handle this thing with DeMarcus the way you want it done. We'll fly home on Sunday night and you and I will sit down and talk to him. Okay?"

"Sounds like a plan." They hung up the phone, but before Demetrius could find something to watch on TV, his cell rang again. This time it was his father.

Demetrius answered, not by saying hello, but by asking, "How long am I going to be babysitting tonight?"

"It's done," Don told him.

"What's done?"

"Not what, but who?" Don responded.

"So, Russ gave you good information?" Demetrius glanced over at the man, who was still sweating like a waterfall.

"Yeah, he did. Now I need you to take him for a drive and then come back to my house for the night."

Demetrius knew that his dad was asking him to kill Russ. Ten years ago his father had wanted to kill a friend of Demetrius' because he didn't want to pay the money owed on a bet. Demetrius had skipped town with his old friend so that his father couldn't get to him. His father chased after them and had almost died during a freak accident. Al had called Demetrius Judas, but they had eventually let him back into their good graces, sort of, after Demetrius helped to save his father's life… now he was being tested. Could he be a stand-up guy to the family when the chips were down? "I'll take care of it."

Don had a three car garage in which a Mercedes, a Hummer and a 4x4 truck was housed. The dirty work was done in the 4x4. So, Demetrius shoved Russ into the truck and backed out of the garage. As they made their way through back roads, Demetrius turned on the radio. The Power of Love by Luther Vandross was playing. Demetrius smiled as he thought about the love he and Angel shared. They were meant for each other.

Angel's parents were these real religious folks who saw God in the midst of everything. Demetrius didn't agree with them, because he lived in his father's world where something bad could happen at the drop of a dime… how could God be in the midst of that? But he did believe that God had brought him and Angel together. Because there was simply no other way to explain how he had come upon her in that alley, at just the right moment, to save her from a creep like Frankie Day.

He turned up the radio and was about to start singing along, when a news broadcaster interrupted the broadcast with a breaking news story. The newscaster said, "Two dead bodies are laying in the street between third and main in the downtown area. This is the eleventh gang related killing in the city this week and it has put city officials on high alert." Demetrius turned the radio off.

Russ turned to him and said, "Your father must have killed Michael Crain. I guarantee you he's one of the bodies in the street."

"You told him where to find the man, so what did you expect?"

"I didn't expect any of this, man. All I was trying to do was score enough cash to keep my girl from getting evicted and then put some food on the table like a man is supposed to do."

"Is a man supposed to get a job? Why didn't you try doing that rather than coming for me and my family?"

"Who's going to give a job to a felon?" Russ screamed out the words. "I messed my life up. I know that. But does that mean that my kids don't deserve a place to lay their head or food in their stomach?"

If his kids were going hungry, Demetrius would be desperate to fix the problem as well. DeMarcus was hurting because of his and Angel's actions and Demetrius was desperate to solve that problem as well. So, he understood where Russ was coming from. "Is Russ your real name?"

"Full names Russell, but most people just call me Russ," he answered Demetrius and then said, "If I had money I'd give it to you. But I don't have nothing… but you know what. My kids' eyes still light up when I come home. Please don't take me from them."

The guy was begging for his life. Demetrius didn't understand this, because he would have taken him out and then collected his earnings without thinking twice about Demetrius' kids. "Let me ask you something, Russ. If you woke up tomorrow morning, would you be thinking about picking up a gun to earn a quick buck, or what would you do?"

"I've been thinking about this every since your father busted in on us. I ain't never been much. My mama washed her hands of me the last time I got arrested. But my girl has stuck by me. She's been pushing me to make a change. Last week she brought home some registration papers for this technical program."

Demetrius had a woman in his life who pushed him to do better also, so again, he identified with Russ. "Yeah, what kind of program is it."

"I'm good with my hands. I can fix anything. So she's got it in her head that I could become a mechanic. So, that's what I'd do if I woke up tomorrow. Right after I kissed my kids good morning. I'd fill out those papers and get myself a trade." Russ nodded his head as he said words that sounded real good to him. "I just wish I had listened to her, and kept myself at home instead of running the streets."

Demetrius stopped the car, then leaned over and untied Russ. A slight whimper escaped Russ and he ducked his head as if trying to escape a bullet. Demetrius pointed toward the Greyhound bus station that was in front of them. "Consider this your lucky day."

Russ looked out the window, he then turned back to Demetrius. "You're letting me go?"

"I need you to listen to me real good if you don't want to wind up dead."

"I'm listening." His eyes began to water and he wiped it away.

"You can't ever come back to this town, not ever. If you do, both of us will suffer," Demetrius told him. "Now I'm giving you the opportunity to become the man your girl believes you can be, and to raise your children. Don't make me regret this."

"I don't know what to say."

Demetrius took a wad of cash out of his pocket and handed it to Russ. "This should be enough to get you to another city and for you to bring your family. Send them a bus ticket when you get where you're going. Then use the rest to pay for rent on a place for a few months."

Russ shook his hand. "You won't regret this, Demetrius. From this moment forward, Russell Parker is going to be a better man."

Saul was outside of the Greyhound bus station. He was pushing a cart like a homeless man. As Russ tried to pass by him, Saul bumped him with the cart.

Russ stopped and said, "Hey man, watch it."

"Sorry about that. I'm so hungry, I'm not paying attention to where I'm going."

"I know how that is, man." Russ pulled a five off of his stack and handed it to Saul. "Get yourself a sandwich or something."

Before taking the money, Saul shook Russ' hand. "For this kindness, God will bless you. Now go and sin no more."

Russ felt something strange shake through his body. It was a weird feeling, but he shook it off and headed inside the Greyhound so he could get out of town before Don Shepherd caught up with him.

Saul watched Russ walk away, confident in the knowledge that the young man would turn his life around. He wanted to smile, but as he glanced over at Demetrius driving off, Saul's lips couldn't form a smile, because he knew that life was about to take a really bad turn for Demetrius and his family.

Nine

The plane was leaving at three o'clock. Angel's parents were going to drive them to the airport right after church. Angel had wanted to sleep in, but the boys were excited about going and KeKe wanted to attend a service at Full Gospel Church before they all left town.

It seemed strange to Angel that KeKe was so excited about attending her parent's church because she wasn't a church goer. But in the week's time that they had been at her parent's home, KeKe had spent a lot of time with Angel's mother, Maxine. Now KeKe was walking around with a bible, clutching it like it was silver and gold.

"Girl, why on earth are you carrying that bible around?"

"You're mom gave me this bible yesterday. She even had my name engraved on it." KeKe showed Angel the engraving on the front of the bible. "I'm taking it to church this morning."

Yes, her father did preach from the bible, but Angel hadn't bothered to carry a bible to church since she was a little girl. "My mom has her hooks in you. I heard her quoting scripture when y'all were talking yesterday."

"She's a real nice lady. I probably wouldn't be in the situation I'm in now if I had grown up in a Christian household rather than the party house."

"I hear you," Angel said as they left for church. Angel had fell into some dire situations after she had left the safety of her mother's home, so she understood how KeKe was feeling. But what she didn't understand was why KeKe felt the need to go down to the altar at the end of service.

KeKe was crying as she lifted her hands and repeated after the altar worker who was standing in front of her as they prayed together. Angel turned to her mother and whispered, "Did you really have to convert my housekeeper?"

Maxine smiled. "You're next."

~~~~

Demetrius picked his family up from the airport and brought them home. KeKe then took Dee and Dontae to get some ice cream so Demetrius and Angel could talk to DeMarcus. The trio gathered in the family room with a pizza box between them. DeMarcus loved cheese pizza so Demetrius had picked up a large cheese on his way to the airport. It was a blatant attempt to butter the boy up, but at this point he was willing to do whatever he had to do.

While DeMarcus was eating his first slice, Demetrius cleared his throat and then said, "First thing I want to do is apologize to you, son." Angel put her hand in his. Demetrius squeezed it. "We never should have kept the truth of your birth from you."

Putting his pizza down, DeMarcus challenged Demetrius, "So you're admitting that you're not my father?"

Demetrius body swayed back as if he'd just been punched. "I'm admitting no such thing. I'm your father and I'll always be your father."

"What your daddy's trying to tell you," Angel took over, "Is that he has been in your life even before you were able to walk. The first time you said 'daddy' it was to him. And Demetrius officially adopted you when you were three years old. So, you see, we haven't been lying to you, because he is your father… the only father you've ever known."

"But he's not my biological father?" DeMarcus asked, trying to get them to say the words.

Angel lowered her head. "No baby, Demetrius is not your biological father."

"I knew it… all this time, I knew something was different about me." Tears were flowing down DeMarcus' face as shivered from the pain he was feeling.

Demetrius grabbed DeMarcus and pulled him into his arms. He held tight to the boy and refused to let him go until the tears stopped. "You are my first born son, DeMarcus. Do you hear me? There is nothing different about you. We are a family and I love you."

DeMarcus dried his eyes as he pulled away from Demetrius. "Dee is your first son, not me."

Demetrius shook his head as he pointed at DeMarcus' chest. "Not Dee… you, DeMarcus. You are my first born. I loved you from the moment I saw you. I love all my boys the same. There is no difference."

"You've never treated me different, but I just knew. I don't look like Dee and Dontae."

"Be thankful," Angel tried a joke to lighten the mood. "Look at that big nose on your father's face. You don't need that in your life."

"His nose is kind of big." DeMarcus poked at Demetrius' nose. "Looks just like Grandpa's. All spread out."

"Okay, okay, everybody can't have a perfect little nose… but seriously, DeMarcus, are you okay now?"

DeMarcus did answer for a moment, but then he said, "I feel better about it now that we've talked. But, the thing I don't understand is why my real dad has never come to see me."

"I am your real dad," Demetrius corrected him.

"I know that, Dad. I mean, my biological dad."

Demetrius glanced at Angel, hoping that they were still on the same page with this. Angel patted his shoulder, took a deep breath as she said, "You see son, I'm sure your dad would have come to see you if he could have. But he died, which is the reason Demetrius didn't have any trouble adopting you."

~~~~

KeKe brought the kids back about an hour later. She saw that Angel, Demetrius and DeMarcus had fallen asleep while watching a video in the family room. So, KeKe took the kids upstairs and got them ready for bed. Once she had tucked Dee and Dontae in bed, Dontae said, "Read me a story."

KeKe had dropped out of school in the tenth grade, so she wasn't much of a reader. But she had started reading the bible that Maxine gave her, she was reading the 37th chapter of the book of Genesis. KeKe went to her bedroom and got her bible. She then rushed back to the kids' room anxious to share what she was learning in this wonderful book. She sat down in between Dee and Dontae's twin beds and starting reading where she had left off…

Now Jacob dwelt in the land where his father was a stranger, in the land of Canaan. This is the history of Jacob.

Joseph, being seventeen years old, was feeding the flock with his brothers. And the lad was with the sons of Bilhah and the sons of

Zilpah, his father's wives; and Joseph brought a bad report of them to his father.

Now Israel loved Joseph more than all his children, because he was the son of his old age. Also he made him a tunic of many colors. But when his brothers saw that their father loved him more than all his brothers, they hated him and could not speak peaceably to him.

Now Joseph had a dream, and he told it to his brothers; and they hated him even more. So he said to them, "Please hear this dream which I have dreamed: There we were, binding sheaves in the field. Then behold, my sheaf arose and also stood upright; and indeed your sheaves stood all around and bowed down to my sheaf."

And his brothers said to him, "Shall you indeed reign over us? Or shall you indeed have dominion over us?" So they hated him even more for his dreams and for his words.

Then he dreamed still another dream and told it to his brothers, and said, "Look, I have dreamed another dream. And this time, the sun, the moon, and the eleven stars bowed down to me."

So he told it to his father and his brothers; and his father rebuked him and said to him, "What is this dream that you have dreamed? Shall your mother and I and your brothers indeed come to bow down to the earth before you?" And his brothers envied him, but his father kept the matter in mind.

The next morning during breakfast Dontae asked Demetrius, "Daddy, do you love me more than you love DeMarcus and Dee?"

Angel was handing Demetrius a plate. Her brows furrowed as she looked at her youngest son. "Why would you ask something like that?"

"I just don't want my brothers to hate me because I'm the favorite. If you want, you can love DeMarcus and Dee more than me," Dontae said, as if that solved the whole matter.

"I love all of my boys the same, that's it and that's all," Demetrius said, as he glanced over at DeMarcus who had lowered his head once Dontae started talking about favorites and such. Now Demetrius was angry, all the work he and Angel had put in last night, trying to get DeMarcus to understand that he was just as special as the rest of the kids was being undone with Dontae's comments. "And why are we even talking about senseless stuff like this anyway?"

KeKe was at the stove stirring grits, she smiled as she turned to the group. "I think this is my fault, Demetrius. I read the boys a bible story about Joseph and his brothers last night. And I guess the thought of brothers hating each other must have scared Dontae."

"It should scare him." Demetrius threw his napkin on his plate and stood up. "We are family. One for all and all for one. We don't hate on each other, we make each other better... got me?"

Demetrius was staring down his boys, daring them to question his statement. Dee and Dontae answered, "Yeah, we got you."

Demetrius turned to DeMarcus. "What about you, son? Are you with this family?"

DeMarcus nodded. "All for one and one for all."

Angel sat down to the left of DeMarcus and put an arm around his shoulder. She then kissed her son on the forehead.

"Can I speak to you in the front room, KeKe?" Demetrius asked.

"Sure." KeKe turned off the stove and followed her employer. "What's up?" she asked once she was standing in front of him.

"I didn't know you were reading to the boys at night. When did that start?"

KeKe shook her head. "I don't normally read to them. Angel does that. But you all were stretched out sleep in the family room when I came home with the boys, so I got them ready for bed and then Dontae asked for a story."

"You do know that we have tons of books for story time?" Demetrius asked.

"Yeah, I know that. But I've recently started reading the bible and I thought they would enjoy the story of Joseph."

KeKe was cool people, but he wasn't about to let her destroy his family with all of that bible stuff. So he told her, "I don't want that religious stuff in my house. My sons live in reality, not in the fantasy world that's in that bible."

"But it's not fantasy, Demetrius." KeKe's eyes were glowing as she told him, "I'm so thankful that you and Angel allowed me to go with her to visit her family because I discovered just how real God is, and I just want the world to know about all the joy I've found."

"That's not going to fly in my house. We don't go for religious stuff. So, if you can't stop spreading your joy, then you can't work here anymore."

"Wait, hold on," Angel said as she walked into the room. "You can't fire KeKe over this. I'm the one who suggested that she visit my parents with me. So, if she wants to read her bible and pray and believe in God, that's none of our business, Demetrius."

"I don't want her trying to convert my family into a bunch of mindless bible thumpers," he told Angel.

"And I don't want you saying things like that to our children. You don't believe in God... fine, but don't try to stop the kids from making their own decisions."

Demetrius wasn't having it. He reminded Angel, "Before we got married you promised that you wouldn't bring any of that religious stuff into our home. Now, are you a woman of your word or not?"

Rolling her eyes, Angel turned to KeKe. "This is not about you, KeKe. But my husband," she flicked her eyes toward him and then turned back to KeKe, "is afraid of the Holy Ghost and prayer I guess. So, please just keep your bible in your room and if you read to the kids, just make sure it's one of the books they already have."

Angel then turned back to her husband, "Is that all?"

"Yeah, but you didn't have to make it sound like I'm some big coward or something." Flexing his muscles, Demetrius said, "I'm not afraid of nothing... believe that."

"I know Bae, you're Superman."

"Remember that the next time you want to talk stuff about me being chicken-little." Demetrius opened the front door and walked out of the house as Angel and KeKe started laughing at him.

Ten

One year later…

Business was booming. Don had doubled his shipment of drugs into the Tri-City and Demetrius was working with construction workers, land developers and project managers to build a new complex that would house good quality businesses to serve the West side of Dayton. The influx of drugs was destroying the community, but Demetrius saw this project as his way of giving back. Besides the grocery store, and the cleaners with an attached laundromat, Demetrius was opening a soul food restaurant, hair supply store and a hair and nail salon. His plan was to leave a few empty buildings available for lease, so others could join in.

The only problem that Demetrius was having now was that it seemed as though the cops had a tail on him. When he mentioned this to his father, Don had said, "I'm being followed too."

"Why are the cops watching us? I thought you greased enough palms downtown. I mean… I didn't have any problems getting my permits for construction on our business complex."

Don told him, "One of my informants at the station said that he got hot for us after all that nasty business with Michael Crain. The governor came down hard on the mayor and now they've got to do some police work... just keep your nose clean and they'll move on to something else."

Later that night, Demetrius watched the evening news with Don, Al and Stan. The anchor discussed the mayor's new initiative to take a bite out of crime and then they joined the mayor's press conference where he was saying, *"This city is experiencing a great deal of anxiety due to the influx of drugs and crime. The police don't seem to be able to do anything to stop these drug dealers even after we have used tax payer money to increase the force. So, I'm calling for an investigation into the reported misconduct of our police force. And if any are found to be aiding these drug dealers rather than taking them into custody, then they themselves will be arrested."*

Al shook his head. "Our mayor must be tired of going home to his family every night."

Stan got up and turned off the television. "Yeah, sounds like he's just asking for someone to put a bullet in his head."

Don didn't seem phased. He opened his wall safe, took out several stacks of cash and handed them to Al and Stan. "Start spreading that around to some of our boys in blue, see if that gives them enough incentive to keep their traps shut."

Demetrius began wondering if his father was some kind of evil genius. Because even with the threat of the police breathing down their necks, he kept doing business... kept making money. And suddenly, nobody was following Demetrius or his father for that matter. They backed off and for months, life was good and peaceful again.

But then one day while Demetrius was at the construction site, he caught a guy taking pictures. Demetrius took the man into a trailer that was being used by the project manager and his crew. He asked the crew to leave the trailer as he flung the picture taker into the seat across from him.

"You've got five seconds to start explaining yourself," Demetrius told the man once the crew members had left the trailer.

"What's the big deal? I was just taking a few pictures."

"But you're dressed like our construction workers, so you're supposed to be out their putting my buildings together, not taking pictures. When I see something like that… I tell myself, 'hey, maybe this guy doesn't really work on this site. Maybe he's some kind of mole'." Demetrius pulled his gun out of his holster. "So, I say again, and for the last time. Why are you on my property?"

The man stared at Demetrius for a moment, he then slowly asked, "Can I reach into my jacket pocket?"

Demetrius shook his head. He wasn't about to be caught off guard, by some little dweeb with wire rim glasses and a dollar store jacket on. "I'll get it." Demetrius reached his hand in the man's jacket and pulled out his identification badge. He name was Sterling Smith, and he was special agent with the FBI.

"You're Don Shepherd's son, right?"

Demetrius threw Sterling's identification back at him. "What's it to you?"

Sterling put his badge back in his pocket. "We are investigating your father on charges that I cannot discuss at this moment."

"Then you're at the wrong place. I purchased this land with my own money and my father has nothing to do with it."

"You got the money from your father."

"I received a loan from my father's company and there is nothing illegal about that. So, I suggest you get off my property before I treat you like a trespasser."

Sterling stood, took out a business card and handed it to Demetrius. "If you want to protect yourself and your family, I suggest you think long and hard about getting on the right side of this. Your father is finally going down. But you don't have to go down with him."

"Get out!" Demetrius yelled and then took the camera Sterling was carrying and smashed it on the ground.

Once Sterling left, Demetrius took out his cell phone and called his dad. Don picked up and Demetrius said, "We got heat."

"My boy, quit worrying so much. I took care of everything. Them boys in blue won't be bothering us. Not if they want to keep living good and taking care of their families in a way they never could of off that civil slave paycheck."

"I'm not talking about the local police or even the mayor having an ax to grind. I just caught a guy snapping pictures at the job sight. And when I questioned him about it, he flashed his credentials and politely told me that you are going down."

"Oh, now that's different."

And for the first time in Demetrius' life, he heard his father's voice quiver with a bit of fear.

~~~~

When Demetrius arrived home and discovered KeKe sitting in the family room with Angel,   his headache became a migraine. He'd told Angel time and time again that he didn't want KeKe in the house while he was there. Six months ago he'd even give her the money needed to put down on a small three bedroom house she wanted to rent. That way she wouldn't have to be in his house with all that praise the Lord and amen business she had taken to saying at the drop of a dime. KeKe used to be cool people, but Demetrius couldn't even have a conversation with her without hearing the name of Jesus. It didn't bother Angel because she grew up with a couple of religious fanatics.

Demetrius held his head as he asked Angel, "Do we have any pain pills?"

"I'll get them for you." KeKe left the room.

"Why is she still here? I thought we had a deal?" Demetrius said to Angel while squinting and holding his head.

Angel came over to her husband, took his hand and led him to a seat. "Poor baby, you must have had a really hard day. You sit right here and let me bring you some dinner."

"What about KeKe?"

"She only stayed over because she wanted to thank you. Just hold tight and you'll find out what a wonderful thing you did." Angel went into the kitchen and fixed her husband's plate. KeKe had just handed him the pain pills and a glass of water. "Eat this, and then why don't you go lay down. I'll take the kids to practice tonight."

"Thanks Angel. I am tired and would love to get some rest tonight." He then turned to KeKe and said, "And I'm sure you want to get home yourself."

She nodded. "But I couldn't leave without telling you how God used you to bless me and my kids."

There she goes with that God stuff again.

"Now that I have a home, and a new job that will be paying a bit more than I'm making right here, children services has finally agreed to give my children back!" KeKe and Angel hugged each other and started jumping around the room.

But Demetrius was thinking that God hadn't used him at all. He offered KeKe the management position at the soul food restaurant that he was opening to get her out of his house once and for all.

Angel objected to him firing her, but she couldn't object to KeKe getting a better job. So, the deed was finally done. He would have KeKe out of his way once the restaurant opened.

"Did you hear KeKe, Demetrius," Angel asked him. "She's finally getting her kids back. They are going to be a family again."

"Oh yeah, I heard. I'm sorry, KeKe. My head is bothering me so much that I'm not thinking clearly. Congratulations, girl. You straightened your life out and now you get your kids back."

KeKe shook her head and pointed heavenward. "I can't take the credit, Demetrius. If the Lord Jesus hadn't come into my life when He did, who knows what I would have done. I wouldn't have a house, a new job and my kids that's for sure."

"I gave you the money for that house, KeKe, not the Lord." Demetrius lifted his hands in the air and made a trembling motion as he said 'the Lord'.

"Demetrius, leave KeKe alone. She's happy and just wanted to thank you for what you did."

"Well she didn't thank me for what I did. To hear KeKe tell it. The Lord came into our house, put that money in my hands and made me give it to her." He stood up, shaking his head and he went upstairs. "I'm just tired of hearing all this nonsense. I'm going to bed."

"I'm sorry about that, KeKe. Demetrius doesn't mean to insult you. He just wasn't raised in church, so he doesn't understand what you're feeling."

"Don't apologize for me," Demetrius said and then he slammed his bedroom door.

Eleven

The feds picked them up one by one. Al was at the car wash arguing with the manager about a scratch on his sky blue two seater, convertible Mercedes.

"I serviced your car myself, sir. And I promise you that I didn't scratch it."

"Then why didn't you say anything to me about the scratch before you started washing the car?" Al walked around his car, looking for more damage.

The manager looked around, making sure there were plenty of witnesses. "Look, I'm sorry. If I scratched it, then we'll pay for it. Just send the bill to us and I'll get my boss to sign off on it."

Al was about to get in the grill of this manager. He'd just bought his convertible six weeks ago and now this moron couldn't even do his job without scratching up his car. But just as he was about to approach the guy, Al noticed the two suits that had just walked into the waiting area and two other suits that had gotten out of a car that pulled up directly behind his Mercedes. He went for his gun.

But the suits got the draw on him. "Don't do it, Al, FBI."

Stan had just made a drop and was now turning onto his street so he could go home and get some rest when a police siren went off behind him. He looked in his rearview mirror and saw that the officer was directing him to pull over. Stan had not ran a red light. He'd put his signal on before making the turn onto his street. So by all accounts he was just another, law abiding citizen trying to get home without being stopped on the street for driving-while-black. But the police had a real problem with a brother in an Escalade.

Stan pulled over, thankful that he had already gotten rid of his stash. They could search his car if they wanted to, they would find nothing. "What can I do for you, officer," Stan asked as the police officer walked up to his window.

"License and registration."

Stan popped his glove compartment and handed the officer what he requested.

The officer then went back to his car and just sat there. He wasn't calling in Stan's information or checking plate numbers, nothing. Stan smelled a set-up. He wasn't about to sit here and wait on somebody to drive by and shoot him in the head. He turned his car back on and gunned it up the hill. Stan's house was out the bottom of the hill, so he couldn't see it when he first turned onto his street, but as he came down the hill he was seeing plenty now.

His house was surrounded and men with guns were waiting on him. Bullets started firing and his left tire was shot out. Stan lost control of the car and started spinning, until the car tipped over and slid into his driveway.

Somebody must have put a hit out on him, Stan thought as he tried to reach for his glove compartment. But his door was swung open, he was pulled out of the car as several FBI badges were shoved into his face. "Stan Michaels, you're under arrest."

Don was at the Marriott, having breakfast in bed served to him by Stacy. A twenty-two year old he'd met at Spunky's nightclub. He'd been wining and dining her for about a week, so they'd finally made things official last night. As she fed him his eggs and toast, Don was thinking about keeping this one. Maybe he'd even move her in. It was way past time for Lisa to pack her bag and get.

"I'd love to cook for you myself," Stacy told him. "But I can't just bring you to my mom's house for dinner. She'd never understand our age difference."

"Look here, baby, what your mama don't know, won't hurt her. You can cook for me at my house." Then he had another thought. "Better yet, I'll get you an apartment this week. You're too old to be staying with your mama anyway."

"You'd do that for me?" Stacy was beaming as she continued to feed him.

"I take care of what belongs to me." Before Don could say any more sweet nothings he glanced at his plate. "Where are my sausage links?"

Stacy checked out the tray, but didn't see the sausage links. "They must have forgotten them. I'll call room service."

Just as Stacy picked up the phone to call, there was a knock on the door. "Room service."

"Don't tip 'em this time. Because they knew all along they had left my sausages off the plate. If they want to be a top notch establishment, then they have to put in the work," Don said as Stacy opened the door.

There was a smile on his face as he watched her walk. She had a voluptuous body that he was going to enjoy snuggling up to night after night. But the smile left his face as several men burst into his room and handcuffed him.

Demetrius was getting excited. The complex was just about finished and he would be able to begin moving equipment into each store next week. He needed to check on the businesses at the other location to ensure that everything was being packed and that they would be ready for the moving trucks. But as he was about to leave the new complex two plain clothed detectives approached him with guns drawn. "Demetrius Shepherd?" one of them asked.

"Yeah, that's me. What's the problem?"

"You're under arrest sir. Please put down your briefcase so I can cuff you."

"Cuff me? For what? What have I done?"

The badges came out and one of the men was with the FBI. He told Demetrius, "You're being arrested as a co-conspirator in a criminal enterprise and a gang member."

"What gang?" Demetrius was tripping. Co-conspirator he could see, but there weren't any real gangs in this city.

"You are part of the Shepherd gang headed by your father, correct?"

~~~~

They were all in custody now, and the FBI agents had put them in separate rooms in order to try to get one to turn on the other. But all Al told them was his name, address and that he needed a lawyer. Same thing happened when they attempted to interrogate Stan and Don.

Demetrius was the last of the 'gang' to be brought in. He was placed in a hot room by himself for several hours. By the time someone opened the door he was sweating profusely. "What's wrong with the air in this place?' Demetrius asked Sterling Smith as he walked into the room.

"You don't like our little sauna?"

"Not at all," Demetrius told him and then added, "But if you think a little sweat is going to rattle me, you've got another thought coming."

Sterling took the seat across from Demetrius. He looked him in the eye as he said, "This is how it's going to work. We know about the criminal enterprise your daddy has been running for years, but we need someone to put the drugs in his hands. Because we haven't been able to catch him with them.

"Now you can talk and or I can go down the hall to Stan or Al. But I'm telling you now, the first one to talk will get the deal. Everybody else will be headed to prison for a very long time."

Sterling's speech should have shook Demetrius to the core. He should have opened his mouth and started telling everything he knew… but instead he laughed.

"It won't be so funny when you're behind bars, Demetrius. You better wise up and start talking." Sterling stood as if he was about to leave. "Maybe you want me to deal with Stan or Al?"

"Man, why did you think I'm laughing at you. Them guys will never turn on each other. You can go to Stan or Al. Heck, go to Don and ask him to turn on Stan and Al. So, if you arrested us without the evidence needed to put my father away. Then I say good luck, because you'll need it."

Sterling opened the folder he'd brought into the room with him and threw a few photos on the table. Two was of Demetrius shaking hands with suppliers on the job sight. He'd inflated the checked he'd paid to each of those men so Don could use the money to purchase his drug shipments. The next picture was of him and Frankie Day. It was of the day that he'd made Stan's delivery for him because 'the gang' had been busy making funeral arrangements for Joe-Joe.

Demetrius leaned back in his seat, twisted his lip as he stared up at Sterling. "I want to speak with my lawyer."

~~~~

The arrest of the infamous Shepherd gang had been all over the news and during news breaks all day. She'd rushed down to the jail, but had been told that she would not be allowed to see her husband until he was booked and processed through the system.

After waiting for several hours, Angel went to sit in her car so she could call KeKe.

"Did they let you see him?" KeKe asked after the women said their hellos.

"No, I'm still waiting. Evidently they've been holding him for hours without officially booking him."

"That's terrible. I'm so sorry about this, Angel."

"I'm trying to keep it together because Demetrius wouldn't want me to break down in front of those people. But I need to talk to my man. At least hear his voice or something."

"I'll start praying for that right now," KeKe told her.

"Thank you, KeKe. We could use some prayers right now. Also, can you pick the boys up for me and order them a pizza. I'll get home as soon as I can."

"Would it be okay if I picked my kids up and brought them over here too? I don't want to get in trouble with the after school program for picking them up late."

"Of course, KeKe. You don't even have to ask. Please pick them up and let the kids have movie and pizza night."

"Okay, would you like to pray before we hang up?"

Angel shook her head. "I'm so worn and weary right now, KeKe. I don't even have the strength to pray. Can you please just do it when we hang up?"

KeKe agreed to pray. They hung up and Angel dropped her head against the headrest and stared out the window. Life had been good with Demetrius. He'd promised to take care of her and he'd done just that. He promised to get a legit job so she wouldn't have to worry about the police coming after him, and he'd done that. Demetrius got up every morning and earned his living like a normal law abiding citizen. So, she just didn't understand why the police would take him away from their family. It just didn't seem fair.

Tears streamed down her face as she imagined life without the man she had spent more than a decade with. The man whom she'd fell more and more in love with every single day. This couldn't be happening to them.

Just as she was getting real good into her pity party, her cell phone rang. She didn't recognize the number but quickly answered it and discovered that it was a collect call from Demetrius. "Yes, of course I accept," she told the operator.

"Hey baby," he said, sounding calm and relaxed.

But Angel was nowhere near calm. Her world was being rocked and she wanted answers. "What is going on, Demetrius. Why on earth did they arrest you?" Tears were streaming down Angel's face as she held the phone to her ear.

"Baby, I don't know. They claiming that I'm a gang member and some other crazy stuff that won't hold up in court."

"What kind of gang do they think you're in?" Angel started wiping her eyes. Maybe this was some big mix up and Demetrius would be released and allowed to come home.

"They're calling my father's organization a gang. So, they arrested me, Don, Stan and Al. We need to get a lawyer, baby."

"Okay. I'll start calling around."

Demetrius told her. "These bums are talking all kinds of crazy. They're trying to say that my father owns the complex. And if they can determine that, then they will strip us of our livelihood. I'm not trying to have that."

"But your daddy signed the business over to you. He doesn't have anything to do with it anymore."

"You know that and I know that. But they aren't trying to hear it." Demetrius sounded frustrated. "I thought I was finally building something good for my family and now look."

"Things will always be good for us, Demetrius. Do you hear me? I just need to get you back home and it will be all good."

"I know, Bae... I know."

"When can I see you? I've been sitting down here for hours. But all they keep telling me is that you haven't been processed yet."

"They're playing games. Just go home and be with the kids. And get me a lawyer down here ASAP."

"What about your dad? Does he need a lawyer too?"

"My father probably has a lawyer on speed dial, but the police won't let me see him, so I don't know if he's been able to make a call or not yet. I'm just trying to cover the bases before they stop letting us use the phone or something."

"They can't do that. You have rights as a citizen of this country," Angel said.

"I've got rights alright. That's why they kept me in some hot room for hours trying to sweat a confession out of me."

"I'm scared, Demetrius."

"Don't be scared, Angel. These guys can't prove a thing. We're going to walk out of here. But we're going to need a lawyer to force them to do right by us."

"I'm on it. We're going to fight this together. Do you hear me, Demetrius…? I'm with you, baby."

Twelve

But it was hard to fight when all their assets were being frozen. Angel had made contact with an attorney but he wanted three thousand before he would even meet with Demetrius. When she went to the bank to get the cashier's check, Angel was told that the account was frozen.

"What do you mean... frozen. We put this money in the bank and I need to get some of it now," Angel screamed at the teller.

"Ma'am, I'm sorry, but I can't override our system."

"But I need that money," Angel was pleading with her.

The teller handed Angel back her withdrawal slip and then awkwardly looked away.

Angel put her withdrawal slip in her purse and walked out of the bank with as much pride as she could muster. She sat in her car and called Lisa. She was surprised her mother-in-law hadn't called her after Don and Demetrius had been arrested, but she hadn't heard from the woman. Angel was hoping that Lisa had some big stash that she'd be able to use. But Lisa wasn't answering. Angel had left several messages, but after wasting an entire day waiting on a returned call, Angel figured that Lisa wasn't going to call back.

Angel had no choice, she would have to call her parents. She just couldn't stand to hear the I-warned-you-about-marrying-him sound in her mother's voice, so she immediately decided to call her dad rather than her mom.

Pastor Marvin Barnes picked up on the first ring. "Hey daughter, how is everyone?"

"We're not doing so good, Daddy."

"I don't like the way you're sounding. What's wrong, sweetie? Is DeMarcus still acting out?"

"No Daddy, DeMarcus has been doing great. He's going to be a starter on his high school football team, and he told me that the coach never lets freshmen start." Her voice cracked as tears drifted down her face. "Demetrius has been arrested, Daddy."

"Oh my Lord… what are the charges?"

"They arrested his father and the other men in his father's organization. Then they picked Demetrius up and charged him as if he was a part of the gang. That's what they're calling them up here… a gang."

"I thought Demetrius was managing several different businesses. How does that make him a part of a gang?"

"It doesn't, Daddy. But the police don't care. They've arrested him and frozen our assets, so I can't even hire an attorney to clear his name."

Her father was quiet for a moment, then he said, "I don't want to upset you, sweetheart, but are you sure that Demetrius wasn't working with his father in his criminal enterprise?"

"No Daddy, Demetrius isn't like that. He is a businessman and that's it." She started crying.

"Don't cry hon, this will work out. I'd like to pray with you, is that okay?"

"Daddy, I need money right now, not prayer." She was getting hysterical. "I hate bringing this to you and mom, but I need a loan."

~~~~

Her father wired five thousand dollars. It had been late in the evening by the time she received the money, so another day would go by before she could meet the attorney at his office and pay him. The next morning, Angel felt a bit of relief as she drove to the attorney office. Demetrius would finally have someone on his side, helping him to get out of this mess his father had undoubtedly gotten him into. But as she parked the car, getting ready to head into the office, her cell rang, she answered and accepted another collect call from her husband.

"I've got the money, Bae. I'm getting ready to pay the attorney now."

"Where'd you get the money from? I thought you told me that our accounts were frozen."

"They are, the bank won't let me touch our account. I called my father and he just wired five thousand dollars. He told me if we need more, he can send another five as well."

"Why did you tell your parents about this? You know what they already think of me. I can't believe you did that."

"Look Demetrius," anger was bubbling up and she was about to explode if he didn't back up. "You need an attorney and our children need to eat, so don't give me any grief about calling my parents."

"Well, it was a wasted call anyway. Because my father's attorney has finally got us arraigned. So, don't give that attorney the money. I'll be in court in the morning for the arraignment and then will know what's going on."

"Okay Demetrius, I'll be there in the morning. Hopefully, they'll let me see you."

"And give that money back to your parents. We don't need their handouts." Demetrius hung up the phone.

Angel loved her husband, and she respected him. But he was in jail and their accounts were frozen. As she drove back home, Angel made up her mind to keep the money. She planned to pay her parents back anyway, but that wouldn't happen until her world got turned right side up again. So, Angel figured that what Demetrius didn't know, wouldn't hurt him.

She went home and took care of the kids. Demetrius had been locked up for two days and the kids kept asking for him. Wondering where their father was and when he was coming home. Angel was running out of excuses so she fed the kids, had them take their baths right after dinner and then allowed them to bring their sleeping bags into the family room and allowed them to do a Thursday movie night. She put DeMarcus in charge of the movies and then went upstairs and climbed into bed, alone.

Angel didn't bother turning on the lights or the television. Tonight, she preferred the dark, it matched her mood. The darker it got outside, the more she fell into depth of depression until she could do nothing but cry and cry and cry.

"Mama, are you okay," DeMarcus asked after knocking on her door.

She grabbed some tissue from her nightstand. Wiped her face and blew her nose. "I'm okay honey, just go back to bed."

DeMarcus opened the door as he said, "But I can hear you crying. Tell me what's wrong, Mama."

Angel sat up as DeMarcus walked over to her bed and sat down on her side of the bed. She couldn't form words for her son, so she lowered her head as more tears fell. Life wasn't supposed to kick her in the gut like this.

"Are you crying because Dad's in jail?"

"Who told you that?" Angel angrily grabbed at the tissue box.

"Kids at school… they said that grandpa was finally getting what was coming to him and that my daddy isn't so lucky to be Don Shepherd's son now."

Angel opened her arms for DeMarcus, he scooted closer and allowed her to wrap her arms around him. "Kids can be so mean. But I don't want you listening to a word they say. Because your daddy is innocent and he will be coming home to us real soon."

"When is he coming home, Mama. We miss him… and I know you miss him too."

"He goes to court in the morning. Hopefully, they'll let him come home then."

"Maybe we should call grandma and ask her to pray for Daddy."

"They're already praying, DeMarcus. Trust me, everything is going to work out. Your daddy is coming back home and this family is going to be just fine. Now go on back to bed so you can get up for school in the morning."

"I'd rather go to court with you," DeMarcus told her as he headed for the door.

But Angel shook her head. "Your daddy wouldn't want you to see him like that." She was thankful that DeMarcus didn't argue the point. He might be built like a linebacker, but at fourteen he was still very much a boy.

She shut her eyes and tried to get to sleep. She told DeMarcus that Demetrius might be coming home tomorrow, but in truth she didn't know what to expect from this arraignment. Angel just didn't want to breakdown in front of her husband. She had to be strong for Demetrius, so that meant, she had to sleep.

This was the first time Angel had laid eyes on her husband in almost a week and he was in handcuffs. She let out a whimper. But when he turned to her, she put her fist to her mouth, because she wanted so desperately to be strong for him.

"I'm okay," he mouthed to her.

Angel nodded. Then the bailiff read off the charges, which made Demetrius sound like some big time gangster. That honor belonged to Don, who was also in the courtroom, but hadn't been brought up for his arraignment yet.

"How do you plead?" the judge asked Demetrius.

Angel wanted to stand up and shout 'not guilty' for him. But she patiently waited as he said, "Not Guilty, Your Honor."

Good, now just give me my husband and let us go home, Angel mind was firing on all cylinders. She'd brought their mortgage papers with her, because she hoped that she would be allowed to hand over the house in trade for her husband, because she had nothing else.

But then she heard the prosecutor say, "Your Honor, we're asking that the defendant be remanded without the possibility of bail. His ties to the Shepherd organized crime family prove that he has sufficient means at his disposal. So, we believe that he is a flight risk."

What was this man talking about? Angel wanted to scream at him.

But she didn't have to because Demetrius' attorney began by saying, "What means... the man's bank account has been frozen. He didn't even have money on hand to retain my services. As far as being a flight risk. My client has significant ties to this community... his wife, his kids, his business."

"Okay, okay, I get it," the judge said. "Bail is set at half a million dollars."

Thirteen

Angel burst out of the courtroom and made a beeline for the bathroom. She pushed open the stall door and threw up in the toilet. Where on earth was she supposed to come up with a half a million dollars? Their home was only worth two hundred and seven five thousand and they still owed a hundred and fifty on it. But she couldn't break down, not now. She had to see this through.

Angel wiped her mouth and headed back into the courtroom just in time to hear the two million dollar bond placed on Don. Her father-in-law seemed to smirk at the judge as if he burned millions of dollars each week because he didn't have enough room in his wallet for all those little bills.

Don really got on her nerves. He was bigger than life, everybody else was beneath him. He even thought he was above the judge and the whole judicial system. She still remembered how Don had punched Demetrius simply because he'd rescued her from Frankie. But Don hadn't cared that Frankie had been trying to pimp her out. He'd only cared about that to save her from Frankie, Demetrius had to leave five thousand dollars on the table.

When she was finally allowed to see Demetrius, she told him flat out that he needed his own attorney. "Your father is not interested in what's best for us... he's always only cared about his own interests."

"Slow down, Angel. We've got to stick together, that's the only way we're going to get through this. Did you hear the bail amounts? No way can we come up with that money on our own. Not since they've frozen our accounts."

"Then what are we going to do, Demetrius? Because me and the kids want you back home."

"Dad will think of something. We've got to trust him on this."

"We can put the house up... maybe the business too, if the feds will allow it," Angel was thinking out loud. Trying to figure a way to get out of this nightmare.

"No!" Demetrius' voice boomed. "You will not put our home up. I'm not going to leave you and the boys without a place to lay your head."

When her visitation time was up, Angel pulled herself out of her seat and headed home, without her husband. She felt hollow and weak as reality was beginning to set in. Demetrius was in serious trouble and he could go away for a very long time.

Her kids were standing at the door waiting as she entered the house. "Where is he?" Dee asked.

Angel's shoulders slacked. "He's not coming home right now. I'm sorry boys. I didn't think he'd be away from us this long either."

"But you told me that he was coming home with you today," DeMarcus said.

"I... I." Angel dropped her purse as she looked around the room, looking for some way out of this conversation. Demetrius was lost to her... he was lost to their boys. She was powerless to do anything about what was happening and all she could do was cry and hug her boys.

They hugged their mother and cried... cried.... cried.

~~~~

On the third day after the arraignment, Angel was getting dressed to go downtown for visitation with Demetrius, when she received a collect call from Don. She almost hung up the phone, but then thought better of it. What if something has happened to Demetrius? She accepted the call. Don tried to butter her up with small talk about the kids, but Angel told him, "I'm in a rush, Don. What can I do for you?"

Don said. "I need you to be a team player, Angel."

"What's that supposed to mean?"

"Prison is a dangerous place and the longer Demetrius is behind bars, the closer he comes to death each day."

Panic struck her. She couldn't move, couldn't think for a moment. She shook herself and asked, "Did something happen to Demetrius?"

"Listen to me, Angel. You are going to have to get the money down here to bond us out."

"What? How? We have no money."

"Frankie owes me. So, I need you to go to him and tell him that I said it's time to pay up. Tell him... if he wants to continue our association, he'll get down here with that money."

Angel gasped. "I can't do that. Demetrius would go through the roof if he knew I was even in the same room with Frankie, let alone asking him for money."

"You can and you will. What Demetrius don't know want hurt him."

"Isn't there someone else who you could turn to for that kind of money?"

"Yeah, but they're locked up with me. The feds stuck it me, Stan and Al real good. But this ain't the end of the story. Not if Frankie can bond us out of here."

"Why don't you send Lisa to Frankie?"

"I would if I could," Don admitted. "But that skank took the money out of my wall safe and hightailed it out of town after my arrest... you just can't trust some women."

Angel wanted to remind Don how poorly he'd treated his wife, but she doubted anything would sink in. Anyone who wronged Don was just wrong and that was that. "Find someone else, Don. I can't do it." She hung up the phone and finished getting dressed.

~~~~

Demetrius had just stepped out of the shower and was immediately punched in the eye by one guy then another gut punched him. He stepped out of the punch like a boxer and went to swing as he'd been trained to do when he worked as a bill collector for his father's loan shark business. He got one guy down on the ground and started pummeling him.

The other guy ran out, leaving his partner in crime to take all that Demetrius was dishing out.

When he realized that his help had left and that Demetrius was still pounding on him, as the guy's head crashed with the cement floor, he yelped, "Don't kill me. I was only following orders."

"What?" Demetrius lifted the guy up by his collar. "Whose orders?"

"Your dad wanted to make sure you could take care of yourself in here."

Demetrius was so angry that he wanted to hit this dude again and again. But if a guard came in here and caught him in the act of killing, Demetrius would get another charge. He didn't need that in his life. Not when his wife was on her way to see him. He released the guy's shirt and let him bump his head on the ground again.

"Don't forget to tell my father what you found out," Demetrius said as he stepped over the man. He then looked at his face in the mirror. His face was puffy and his left eye was starting to close up on him. His dad had picked the perfect time to test him. Now, what was he going to tell Angel?

~~~~

Angel sat at the table with a baggie full of change in case Demetrius wanted a snack out of the vending machines. The first time she'd come, she hadn't known to bring change, but she was getting the hang of prison visitation procedures.

The door opened and Demetrius walked in. He had his head down, so Angel stood up to wave him over to where she was sitting. But a guard immediately told her, "Sit back down."

The angry tone of his voice and the fact that a gun was strapped to his hip scared Angel. She quickly sat back down and waited for Demetrius to join her. Once he was standing in front of her, Demetrius pulled Angel out of her seat and wrapped his arms around her.

"You know the rules, Demetrius. No touching," the guard instructed.

Demetrius eyed the guard as if daring the man to say another word to him. But Angel wasn't as bold. She pulled her husband's hands from around her waist and sat down. "We have to follow the rules, Demetrius. You don't want to get in anymore trouble do you?"

"I'm just happy to see you, Baby. They got me locked up in this hole. I can't see my kids and can't even touch you." Demetrius just shook his head.

That's when Angel noticed his eye. "What happened to your face?"

"Nothing baby, nothing at all. I just fell coming out of the shower."

"How did a fall do that to your eye?" It was purple and blue around the bottom, the top and bottom lids were swollen and half shut.

"I think I scrapped it against something as I tried to brace for the fall." He waved away any thought about his eye. "It's nothing. I'd rather talk about the kids. How are they doing?"

"If you want the truth, they're distressed. Kids are talking about your arrest and they're hearing things, especially DeMarcus."

"Tell them to stop listening to all that crap. And when I get home, I'll make sure they know the truth."

"When will that be, Demetrius? I need to tell the boys something or they are going to start freaking out. You have never been away from home this long and they are getting scared." Angel started crying.

Demetrius tried to comfort her, but there was nothing much he could do. He couldn't tell her when he was coming home because he had no idea how to raise all that money. So, by the time Angel returned home from her visit, she was drained and wanted to beg KeKe to stay a little bit longer, but she wouldn't deprive her of spending time with her own children. Not after all she'd gone through to get them back.

Pizza was on the menu again tonight. The boys were all smiles as they ate. Angel told DeMarcus to clean up and then turn on the television for his brothers. She went upstairs and climbed in the bed, needing a few moments to herself. But just as she was about to close her eyes, the phone rang.

It was another collect call from Don. After accepting the call he asked her, "Did you see Demetrius' face?"

"Yes, I did. He said he slipped coming out of the shower."

"That's not what happened, Angel. Two goons attacked him. They tried to take him down. Demetrius fought them off this time. But who's to say if he'll be able to survive another attack."

Why was this happening? Her husband wasn't supposed to be in jail. He wasn't supposed to be getting attacked and watching his back. He was a businessman plain and simple. She asked Don. "Why did they arrest Demetrius? He's not a part of your organization. He runs his own businesses."

"I foot the bill for those businesses in case you forgot. Demetrius' hands are dirty too, so if I can't get the money to get us out of here... he's going down with the rest of us."

"No, they will figure out that Demetrius doesn't do the things you and your friends do."

"Wake up, Angel. Demetrius does what I tell him to. I don't want to spell this out for you, but believe me when I tell you that Demetrius has just as much reason to worry as the rest of us."

So, Demetrius had been lying to her. He wore a suit and tie to work every day, but he was still a part of his father's organization. Sighing, she said, "Why couldn't you just leave us alone?"

"If I left y'all alone, you, Demetrius and the kids would starve to death. How do you think you got that nice house... those nice cars and all the money you get to spend even though you don't work outside the house?

"You want me to thank you for what you've done to us?"

"Not to you, but for you... and I don't need thanks. But I do need you to be down. And if not for me, for Demetrius. He won't survive in here much longer."

She was in a no win situation. If she didn't do what Don wanted, Demetrius could get hurt again. But if she did it, Demetrius may never forgive her for going behind his back. "I'll do it on one condition."

"What's that?" Don asked.

"I need you to tell Demetrius that you sent me after this money."

"Whatever you want... just go remind Frankie who his friends are."

The next morning as Angel and KeKe drank coffee and ate breakfast in the kitchen, Angel told her about the bruises she saw on Demetrius during her visit.

"And Don told you that he got jumped?"

"That's what he said. So, now Don wants me to tell Frankie to post their bonds." Angel shivered. "I can't deal with the thought of being in the same room with Frankie again."

"You want me to go with you?" KeKe offered.

If it wasn't for the fact that Frankie was a drug dealer and that KeKe was trying her best to stay away from that stuff, she would have jumped at the chance to take KeKe with her. But she couldn't do her friend like that. That's how she thought of KeKe. They were no longer worker and employer... they were friends. She wouldn't have been able to get through all of what she was going through without her girl. "I appreciate your offer, but this is something I've got to take care of on my own."

"Frankie is slimy, but I can't see him ignoring a request from Don." KeKe got up and started dancing around the room. She

104

encouraged Angel to lift her hands. "Come on girl, let's praise God. You're about to get your man back."

"I'm not praising about nothing. When I see Demetrius walk through that door again, then I'll get up and dance and praise with you."

"Faith without works is dead," KeKe told her quoting a bible scripture that encourages all believers to trust God even before they see the promise of what they are waiting for.

The smile that had been on Angel's face disappeared. She remembered that scripture. Her father had quoted it often when she was a child. "I'm just not there yet," she told KeKe honestly.

KeKe sat back down. "I didn't meant to make you sad. I was just happy that you were smiling again. But if I took it too far, then I'm sorry."

"Don't worry about it. What you said just took me back to when I was a little girl and I believed all that stuff." Angel got up from the table and went upstairs to get dressed so she could meet with the devil.

Fourteen

Angel drove over to the home that she had once lived in with Frankie Day. That awful experience had occurred thirteen years ago. And in that space of time she had never drove by this house, not even once. There were no sweet memories lingering around for her.

She had been a sixteen year old runaway when she'd had the misfortune of getting tangled up with Frankie. Back then he had owned a strip club, that he falsely called a 'gentlemen's club'. Frankie had wined and dined her, whispered sweet nothings in her ear, told her how much he loved her. Then Angel had gotten pregnant. By the time DeMarcus was born, Frankie had two other women and he'd moved both of them into the house with her and DeMarcus.

When Angel told him that what he was doing wasn't right, he sent her to stay at his sister's house and then told her she'd have to earn her keep by working at his 'gentlemen's club'. Frankie had even refused to buy DeMarcus' diapers. And he'd threatened to stop paying his sister's bills if she fed Angel or DeMarcus. In her mind, she had no choice, it was either strip or watch her baby starve to death. So, she gave in and started dancing at the club.

Angel became one of the best attractions at the club. Men would come in and offer to take her on trips, buy her a house, all sorts of crazy things. But they just wanted to get close to her and the truth was, they made her skin crawl. Many nights after her skit was finished, she'd go back to the dressing room and cry her eyes out. A stripper named Bambi had offered her some drugs once. Angel had been tempted to take them, because she desperately needed to escape from her miserable life. It was only thoughts of DeMarcus, knowing how much her son needed her, that kept her away from drugs.

She had run away from what she thought was a bad situation with her parents only to run into a demon like Frankie. Angel thought things couldn't get much worse than they were the night she contemplated taking drugs. But Frankie showed her just how wrong she had been the night he tried to prostitute her in order to pay off a debt he owed to Don Shepherd.

Angel will forever be thankful that Don sent Demetrius to collect on the debt that night. Frankie had hit her as she was trying to escape, and Demetrius happened upon the scene and saved her. Now, she would have to deal with Frankie one more time, but it was so she could return the favor to Demetrius, because now he needed her to save him.

She got out of her car and headed towards the door. From what she'd been told, Frankie had moved himself into some big house on the South side of town once he started dealing big drugs to the kids on the street. But he'd kept this house, and from what she'd been told, Frankie was here most days handling business. She knocked on the door and waited.

As the door was opening, Angel felt her skin crawl. She should have taking her allergy pill, because she was definitely allergic to all things Frankie. "Yeah?" the short and stocky man said as he held the door close to his chest.

"I'm here to see Frankie."

"Did he know you was coming?"

"Just tell him Angel is here." Angel turned her back to the door as the man closed it. Frankie was a pig, but he wouldn't turn her away. Not now that she needed his help. Frankie wouldn't be able to resist rubbing her nose in the fact that she needed something from him.

The door opened again and Frankie stood there smirking at her. "Just couldn't stay away, huh?"

She ignored him. "I need to speak with you. Can we do this in private please?"

He opened the door wide and ushered her in. The living room was just as tacky as she remembered with leopard print furniture and portraits of big boob women on the wall. Two men sat on those sofas counting money and passing a joint.

"Follow me," Frankie told her as he took her to a room in the back of the house.

As he closed the door, she told him, "Look Frankie, I can't stay long. Don sent me to talk to you."

"How is DeMarcus?" he asked.

"What?" A look of confusion on her face. "Why do you want to know?"

"He's my son." Frankie pounded his chest. "Chip off the 'ol block. That boy is going to be a football superstar. And he got those genes from me. But you and Demetrius won't even allow me to say two words to my own flesh and blood."

She scoffed at him. "Your son? Aren't you the same man that denied DeMarcus food and diapers until I agreed to strip for you? A father wouldn't do that to his own child. And Demetrius never has. That's why he is the only man DeMarcus will ever call daddy."

"You need to stop lying Angel, because you know I wouldn't have let my son starve."

"I was there, Frankie. And I haven't forgotten a thing that you did to me or DeMarcus."

Frankie waved a hand in the air as if that could take away the past. "You crazy, girl. You're just trying to make me look bad in front of DeMarcus. I would have fed that boy. You was young and dumb, and I just told you that so you could get on that pole like you was supposed to do."

Rolling her eyes heavenward. "I'm not here to discuss the past. Don needs you to post bail for all of them. He sent me here to remind you who your friends are. Because if it wasn't for Don, you wouldn't have the money you have now."

"Yeah, and if it wasn't for Don sending his son to collect on my debt that night, I'd still have my son. And he'd be calling me daddy and thanking me for all his skills on the football field."

Angel wasn't just scoffing, she was full on laughing in his face. "You are pathetic," she told him once she could control her laughter. Frankie was the worst. She was glad that Demetrius had convinced her to tell the courts that Frankie was dead when they filled out the adoption papers. She had had enough. Angel had done what Don asked her to and now she wanted to get as far away from Frankie as possible. "I'm leaving. You can go downtown and visit Don if you need any other information."

But as she tried to walk past him, Frankie shoved her backward, and then bolted the door. "I'm not finished with you," he said while unbuttoning his pants.

"What are you doing? Let me out of here?"

"Let's see if you think this is funny," he said as he attacked her.

Angel screamed and yelled for someone to help her. But no one would help her. The only one who'd ever saved her from anything was locked up in jail right now. And she was trying to save him, when she couldn't even save herself. When she could think of nothing else to do, she bit down on Frankie's shoulder so hard that she drew blood. She didn't even care if it killed her. That would be better than what he was already doing to her.

Frankie yelped like a dog. He smacked Angel and then got off of her. He put his pants back on, took some money out of his wallet and threw it at her. "Make sure you get my son something to eat with that."

He unlocked the door, Angel gathered her stuff and then walked out of the room with as much dignity as she could muster. But then Frankie said, "Tell Don, I haven't forgotten who my friends are. I'll get him right, but that back stabbing son of his can rot in prison for all I care."

It had all been for nothing. Frankie had humiliated her one last time and Demetrius was going to stay in prison. Something snapped in Angel at that moment. She went into the kitchen, opened the draw and grabbed the biggest butcher knife she could find. "You are dead, Frankie. Do you hear me? You're dead." She chased him with the knife.

As he was trying to get away from her, he tripped on one of his leopard print rugs. Angel was on him. She tried to plunge the knife in his heart, but he jerked and the knife went into his arm. She pulled the knife out and tried to stick him again.

Frankie yelled, "Get this crazy girl off of me."

As Angel kept trying to stab Frankie, she felt herself being pulled away from him. "No, no, no. I'ma killing him. Let go of me."

One of the men pulled the knife out of her hand. The other opened the front door and threw her out. She got up and kicked at the door. Then she picked up some rocks and threw them at the windows, breaking at least two of them. Once she saw the window break it was as if all of the adrenaline she'd used to stab Frankie and left and she was suddenly very tired.

She got in her car, wanting to sit there and just cry. But she couldn't stand to be near this house one second longer. So, she called KeKe and asked her to pick the kids up and then drove herself home. Angel then stood under the shower for so long that her skin started to shrivel. Angel turned off the water, put on her pajamas and then climbed into bed.

She was filled with hatred for not only Frankie but for Don as well. Because the more she thought about it, Angel figured that Don had most likely sent her to Frankie as a gift... get me out of jail and you can borrow my daughter-in-law. He'd done it to his own wife, so why would Angel have thought that his daughter-in-law would be any better. The man was unscrupulous and she wanted him dead too. Maybe someone in prison would do her that favor.

Angel was so angry and fuming that she didn't even realize that she was crying until KeKe came into her room and asked if she could do anything to help her.

Angel shook her head, but then she asked, "Can you and your kids stay here tonight? I don't think I'm able to take care of my kids." More tears ran down her face. "I-I just can't do it."

KeKe rushed to her side. "What's wrong, Angel? Did something happen to Demetrius?"

Sitting up in her bed, Angel pulled the cover tight against her body as if that could protect her from the reality of what she'd endured. "I don't know what to do, KeKe."

"You're scaring me, Angel. Please tell me what's wrong. Did something happen at Frankie's place?"

"He raped me," the words were barely a whisper. Angel wrapped her arms around her knees and rocked back and forth. "Demetrius is going to hate me."

"No Angel, this is not your fault. Demetrius won't hate you for this. Matter-of-fact, you don't have to tell Demetrius what happened. Frankie won't be bragging about it. He'd be too afraid of what Don might do."

"Don sent me to Frankie. He's just as guilty for what happened to me. And you know what? I doubt if Don would even care because he's getting his bail money." Angel put her hands over her face and let the tears roll again.

KeKe clung to her friend trying her best to soothe the pain. She started singing, "The storms of life will blow, they're sure to come and go… but the captain of my soul… he rocks me in his arms."

"That's Yolanda Adams… *Through the Storm*, right?" Angel said while the tears continued to fall.

"It seemed appropriate."

"Yeah," Angel agreed. She then turned to KeKe and asked, "Why does God allow storms in people lives anyway? Why do we have to go through so much?"

"I don't know," KeKe answered honestly. "But the one thing I do know is that without my struggles in life, I probably wouldn't have been ready to receive God into my life when your mom presented Him to me. So, I'm okay with everything I went through, because I came out of it and I'm now in a place of peace."

Angel shook her head. "The way I'm feeling right now… I don't see how I can ever find peace again. I stabbed Frankie today. I tried to kill him and I would have if those guys hadn't pulled me off of him."

"Other people were in the house?" KeKe looked as if she was going to be sick.

"Two others. They heard me crying and begging for help, but wouldn't do anything to help me. But they sure stopped me from plunging that knife into Frankie's heart."

"This is bad," KeKe said, while pacing the floor.

"Don't you think I know that? Didn't I just tell you what Frankie did to me?"

"I know that was bad," KeKe tried to explain. "But I didn't know that anyone else was in the house. People don't like being labeled as snitches, but they snitch all the time. Word will be on the street about what happened to you before the night is over."

"So, you think Demetrius will know what happened even before he gets out of jail?"

KeKe nodded. Her hand went to her mouth, this was going to be bad.

Fifteen

In between the time of Angel's attack and Don, Stan and Al's release from jail, which was only two days... word had spread amongst the hustlers in the county jail. They whispered about what Frankie did to Angel and how Angel had tried to stab Frankie to death. Don knew it was all true when Frankie didn't post Demetrius' bond and he was sick over it.

The fact of the matter was that Don had no choice. He had to get himself bonded out or get murdered in prison. The men he dealt with wouldn't just shake their head and feel sorry for him that he was now a prisoner. They were irrational beings who killed over the bottom line. And if he wasn't out of jail and able to take the next shipment, his friends in Columbia would come calling. Demetrius and his whole family would be wiped out, if the Columbians thought there was any chance that Don might talk in prison... or that they had lost their golden child. Don didn't know which might set them off the most, and he didn't want to find out.

So, yeah, he sent Angel to Frankie. But despite what anybody thought of him, he never dreamed that Frankie would have the nerve to touch her. If it hadn't been for Don, Frankie would still be trying to make ends meet with that hole in the wall stripe club he used to own. But Don had taken him under his wing, even floated him the money on his first shipment, so Frankie could start making things happen on the street.

Don and the boys needed to make plans for the shipment that was coming in next week, but before they worked on that they got busy trying to find another hustler who could carry Frankie's load because he wasn't going to be needing it.

Matter-of-fact, Don was in Frankie's basement right now. Frankie was strung up with his arm tied to a pipe that was connected to the wall. Don sat in a chair waiting on a call from Stan, who was having lunch with two of Frankie's associates, trying to determine if either of them was ready to step up and take over. Don and Stan had no fear that anyone would run to the cops, because their life expectancy would suddenly become very low.

"Can we talk about this, Don? Come on, man. You and I do good business together. You're not going to let some female come between that, right?"

"The female you're referring to is my daughter." Don didn't add the 'in-law' part. Because it didn't matter. Angel had been a part of their family for more than a decade... she'd given him grandchildren. And this piece of crap thought he could use her and do whatever he wanted with her. Naw, it don't work like that.

"But she and I have history, Don. I got a kid with Angel just as well as Demetrius does. And they won't even let me see my own kid." Frankie was breathing hard and rapid as he tried to explain himself. "I just got angry... she was putting me down, acting like I was nothing. I had to show her."

"Oh you showed her alright, and you did it with two goof-offs in your house who were happy to tell the whole story to anyone who'd listen."

"I told them not to say nothing. I promise you, Don. I never wanted word to get out about the little scuffle Angel and I had." When Don didn't respond, Frankie pulled at the rope, trying to free himself. But the pulling was tearing at his skin so he gave up and turned back to Don. "Please don't do this." He whimpered, "I bring in a whole lot of money for you. Come on, man."

Don's cell rang. He answered and listened as Stan told him. "It's a go. Julius is going to partner up with Little Red so they can come up with the money for Frankie's shipment."

Don hung up the phone, put his gun in his pocket. He then walked upstairs and grabbed a butcher knife out of Frankie's drawer. Don hummed as he headed back to the basement, twirling the knife. Killing a man didn't bother Don in the least, he'd been doing it since he was eleven and had been left on the street to fend for himself by his junkie mama. He never thought about the people left behind to mourn the dead... or that there might be another way to solve his problems.

Frankie saw the knife and his eyes bugged out. "I paid your bail, Don. Why you gon' do me like this?"

"I'm just finishing the job my daughter started," he told Frankie as he plunged the knife in his heart and then twisted. "Thanks for the bail money," Don said as he left the knife in him and walked away from Frankie's lifeless body.

~~~~

Demetrius' thoughts were all over the place. He needed to get to a phone, but the guards hadn't come to get him yet. He started banging on the bar and yelling for a guard. After about five minutes, a guard appeared in front of his cell. "What's all this noise about, Shepherd?"

"I need to use the phone. I've been telling y'all that since yesterday."

"What do you want," Demetrius whispered. "My father has already been released, so I can make some things happen. Just get me to a phone, okay?"

The guard looked hesitant, but thought better of it. He unlocked the cell and walked Demetrius out of the holding area. As they headed to the phones, the guard whispered for his ears only. "My mom's sick. I need some extra cash for her hospital bills."

"I'll get you squared away," Demetrius told him as he picked up the phone to call Angel.

She picked up and accepted the call. "Demetrius?"

"It's me."

"Thank God. When I hadn't heard from you, I worried that something else had happened."

Demetrius frowned. "Why are you worried about something happening to me? You're the one I'm worried about."

"You're father told me that you didn't fall getting out of the shower. He said that you got jumped."

Demetrius shook his head. "Don't listen to him, Angel. My father planned the whole thing. He wanted to see if I could take care of myself in here. And I showed them all... so I'm good. You hear me?"

Angel started crying. "He lied to me. If he hadn't got me so scared that something was going to happen to you... then I never would have..."

"You never would have what?" He hadn't wanted to come right out and ask her, but if she was about to confirm what he'd been hearing, then Demetrius was all ears.

"I'm so sorry, Demetrius. I'm just so, so sorry." She blew her nose and then added, "Why did Don do this to us?"

Demetrius was confused. "What are you talking about? What did my father do?"

"He kept calling asking me to talk with Frankie about bailing y'all out. I told him that I didn't want to be anywhere near Frankie. But then you got hurt and Don called me again. He had me thinking that you were about to get killed. So, I had no other choice then to do what he asked."

His father was a hustler through and through. He did what had to be done, even if that meant using his son and daughter-in-law as pons. "Tell me what happened, Angel."

"I can't," she shouted, almost to the point of hysterics. "I just can't."

His heart bled for his wife. She only wanted to love him. But she'd never wanted to have any dealings with his father's dirty deeds. "Stop crying, Angel. I promise that I've got your back on this. I won't let anything else happen to you. Not ever."

"When are you coming home, Demetrius? I haven't been able to get out of bed since… since." She couldn't finish the statement so she simply said, "We need you here."

"I know baby. I'll work something out. Just hold on for me, okay?"

"It's so hard without you, Demetrius. I didn't know it would be this hard."

When they hung up, Demetrius went back to his cell with a heavy heart. His wife was hurting… his family was hurting and his dad was the cause of it all. When Demetrius was a child he'd stood at his mother's gravesite and watched her lowered into the ground, all because Don Shepherd pimped her out to some psycho who didn't care that Demetrius needed his mommy to come back home. And Don had done it again. But this time he'd tried to take Demetrius' wife away from him. If the word that was out was to be believed, Angel had stabbed Frankie after he attacked her. Angel could have been killed doing something like that to Frankie, and then he and his children would have been left alone… just as he had been when he was a kid.

One thing his father had told him on numerous occasions was that when somebody got wronged, somebody had to pay for that. Just before Don was released, Demetrius went to him and asked if he'd heard about what happened to Angel. His father had nodded.

Then Demetrius asked him, "Why would she be at Frankie's house in the first place?"

Don had never admitted to him that he'd sent his wife to Frankie, all he'd said was, "Don't worry about it, Son. He's going to pay for what he did."

The way Demetrius saw it, the tax man was coming for Don Shepherd too. Because at that moment, Demetrius hated everything his father stood for and he had come to the conclusion that he also hated his father. He didn't want the man anywhere near his family ever again.

He sat in his cell stewing for several days. When the anger and disgust that he felt for his father still hadn't subsided, Demetrius knew what he had to do. So the next time he was allowed to make a phone call. He called Sterling Smith.

When the FBI agent discovered it was Demetrius, He snidely asked, "Enjoying your time at the country club?"

"As a matter-of-fact, I'm not. When can we talk?"

Sixteen

Demetrius had no problem with turning rat. As far as he was concerned his father deserved everything he was about to get. But first, he needed to cut a few side deals of his own. "Before I say anything, I need y'all to know how this is going down."

Sterling and the other agent didn't say anything. They were there to listen. Demetrius continued, "I need a get out of jail free card and I want the lean taking off my finances and off of my business."

"You're asking an awful lot," Sterling said while jotting down some notes.

"How can I take care of my family, if y'all got everything hemmed up? You want my father, and I want to provide for my kids. So, what's it going to be?"

"You are aware that we've got enough evidence to put your father away for a long time, even without your help, right?" the other agent said.

"And that's why y'all rushed over here and plopped this shiny tape recorder on the table... because y'all don't need my help at all? Okay then," Demetrius shrugged. "See you in court."

Demetrius was about to get up and ask the guard to escort him back to his cell, when Sterling stopped him. "Let's just say, that if your information is sufficient enough to bring down this crime organization, then I'm sure my boss would have no problem granting your request." Sterling hit the button to turn on the tape recorder. "Let's get started."

"What do you want to know?" Demetrius asked.

"How is Don bringing the drugs into this city? We've had a tail on him and his boys but we still haven't figured it out."

Demetrius leaned back in his seat, enjoying every moment of this. Don was about to get his, special delivery from Demetrius himself. "My father works with a buy-here pay-here car dealer. The cars filled with drugs from the glove compartment, the airbags and even the tires. They have workers who work late at night pulling the drugs out of all the compartments and then the car dealers put the cars on the lot and sales them with missing airbags and substandard tires.

"But before any of that happens, my father or Stan will show up and inspect the vehicles. They make sure that all the cars were delivered and then they sign off on it with the car dealer. If you check the car dealers' records, you'll find a long list of cars that have been signed off on. And my father has never driven one of those cars."

Sterling was fascinated. The criminal mind could come up with so many ways to out-slick law enforcement. But it usually caught up with them sooner or later. "How long has this been going on?"

"About ten years."

"Well I'll be," the other agent said.

"My father has made millions and nobody has ever figured out his little secret. Because he decided years ago that if he got into the drug business, he was going to do it at such a high level, that he would be not just bullet proof, but arrest proof."

"He's gotten away with it for a long time," Sterling admitted. "Probably would have kept on doing his dirty deeds if he hadn't littered the streets with so many dead bodies. The mayor wants him gone. And if you're information pans out. We just may be able to make this case stick."

"He has a shipment coming in next week. Once I have my deal in place, I'll provide you with the car dealer's address."

~~~~

While Demetrius sat in jail waiting to have his shackles loosed, Don was trying to make a move. He and Stan were on the way to check on the shipment that had just arrived. Don was normally gleeful on days like this. They were about to get paid and Don would have money in his pocket again so Stan didn't get the mood.

"What's got you sideways today?"

"I've been trying to talk to Angel, but she won't even take my call… hung up on me three times. Don shook his head.

"Give her some time, Don. The girl has been through a lot."

"I just don't want her thinking that I set that up… like I would use her like that." Don shook his head. "I've done a lot of dirty things in my lifetime. But Angel has been good to my son. I never wanted anything like that to happen to her."

"Once we get this shipment logged in, we'll have more than enough money to pay Demetrius' bond. When we get him out, you can have him to talk to Angel. Demetrius knows how the game goes." They pulled in the back of the buy-here, pay-here lot and got out of the car. Lou was waiting for them with his inventory of cars.

"What it do, Lou?" Stan used his normal greeting with the man they had been doing business with for so long.

Lou normally responded, "I'm do to get paid." and then they would high-five and do a little small talk before getting down to business.

But this morning, Lou didn't have a smile on his face, he eyes darted here and there, and his response to Stan was, "I'm not doing so good today. Think I might have a stomach flu or something."

Don grabbed the inventory sheet from Lou. "Ain't nobody trying to catch nothing. Go on back into your office, Stan and I will inventory the cars ourselves."

"Okay, I'll be right inside, so let me know if you need anything." Lou then went back into his office and started shuffling papers around.

Every once in a while Stan would catch Lou peering out at them as if he thought they were about to steal a car or something. "What's up with that dude?"

Don checked the serial number on a white Camry as he said, "That's your boy. I told you he was weird."

"And you know something else?" Stan said, "He don't look like a man with the flu. I think we need to go. Let's just call him from the car."

Don was checking the serial number on the next car. He glanced up at Stan. "You feeling something?"

Stan pulled his keys out of his pocket and headed for the car. Don followed suit. Something was up and they weren't sticking around to find out. Stan floored it as they tried to get the heck out of dodge. But the trap had already been set. The exit was blocked by cop cars. And the police were outside of those cars with guns pointed at them.

"Stop the car and get out with your hands up."

~~~~

As Don was being picked up and put back behind bars where he belonged, Demetrius was being released from jail. He needed to be home with his family, but his first stop was to Frankie's place. Demetrius knew this was the wrong thing to do, but hate and anger had so consumed him that he could think of nothing else but to kill Frankie Day. For years he and Angel had been living as if the man was already deceased, they'd even stated that fact on DeMarcus' adoption application. Now, Demetrius was going to make it a reality.

He tried both the front and back door. Then a couple of windows but couldn't find entry, and nobody was opening the doors. Demetrius didn't want to start hollering and calling Frankie out, because he didn't want to draw attention to himself. As he stood in the backyard trying to figure a way into the house, Demetrius caught a whiff of a pungent order that was just too stank to describe. But he had smelled it before.

He looked through the kitchen window, but didn't see anything. As he made his way back around the house, Demetrius saw a small basement window. He got down on his knees and peered through the glass. His eyes darted from one corner of the basement to the next. Then as he glanced to the right, he saw it… or rather, he saw him. Frankie's arm were tied to a pipe and there was a knife in his chest. He was dead, dead.

Demetrius went home. His kids were at school but Angel was there, still in bed, looking as if life had dealt her a blow that she wouldn't soon recover from. He climbed into bed with her and held her. Angel was finally able to cry on Demetrius shoulder and she did just that for hours. When she was all cried out, she kissed his cheek and said, "Thank you for coming back to me. Please tell me that I'm not dreaming."

"You're not dreaming, baby. They dropped the charges against me. I'm a free man."

Just when she thought she couldn't cry anymore, Angel found fresh tears. "You're home for good?"

They showered together and then made love for the rest of the afternoon. Demetrius and Angel were back together and nothing and no one would dare to tear them apart again. As Angel rested her head on his shoulder, he rubbed her hair as he told her, "I'm sorry."

"You don't have anything to be sorry about. It was your father who did this to me, and I hate him," Angel

After seeing the dead body of Frankie Day and knowing in his gut that his father had made good on his word, some of Demetrius' anger towards his father had diminished somewhat. But he could understand what Angel was feeling. It had been those same kind of feelings that led him to cut a deal with the feds.

His father was going to do time. The way Demetrius saw it, Don was getting time, not just for his drug running operation, but for what he'd done to Demetrius' mother and now, to his wife.

He patted Angel on the stomach as he scooted out of bed and headed back to the shower. "Let's get dressed. I want to take you and the kids out to dinner."

Seventeen

A week after Demetrius was released from prison, Angel thought things were going well for them. Don was locked up, hopefully, never to bother her again. Demetrius was back to work and their accounts were no longer frozen. Angel had even given her parents back the five thousand they'd sent in her time of need. All was good, but then things started unraveling.

First, the five o'clock news came on while she was in the kitchen cooking dinner. The anchor announced that a body had been taken out of the basement of a house in the Trotwood area. "The man has been identified as Frank Day. His friends called him Frankie."

Angel froze at the kitchen sink. She had been cutting up a whole chicken and her knife fell to the bottom of the sink as the anchor continued, "The police broke down the door this morning after receiving numerous complaints from neighbors about a foul order emanating from the house... Frankie was a notorious criminal who had been arrested on charges that range from domestic violence to drug trafficking. Authorities believe that Frankie's death was a result of a drug deal gone wrong."

DeMarcus came into the kitchen. He pointed towards the television in the other room as he said, "Some man named Frankie Day just got killed."

Angel wished she was a praying woman like KeKe and her mother, because she desperately wanted God to rewind the last two minutes of their lives. She would have turned the TV on a program the kids wanted to watch instead of telling them to stop hogging the TV and let her listen to the news for a few minutes. Or maybe if she had the last fourteen years back, she would have just told DeMarcus then and there that his so-called father was no good and that they wouldn't allow him around an evil person like Frankie for his own good. But she hadn't prayed in years, so Angel was on her own.

"I heard." She picked the knife back up and finished cutting her chicken. Wishing with each cut that she had been the one to deal Frankie his final blow.

"That's my father's name."

Angel swung around, eyes full of hatred, not for DeMarcus, but for the man he dared to call father. "Demetrius Shepherd is your father, and don't you ever forget that. He's the one who puts food in your stomach and clothes on your back. He's the one who loves you like a father should."

"But you lied to me!" DeMarcus yelled at her. "But if you had told the truth I could have at least spent time with my real father before he died."

"Over my dead body!" Angel put the knife down. "I would have never let you spend a day with that evil demon."

"If he was an evil demon, Mama, then what am I?" DeMarcus ran off to his room and slammed the door before Angel could respond.

She wanted to chase after DeMarcus so she could explain herself. But she felt her lunch rising and had to run to the bathroom instead. Demetrius picked the exact moment when Angel had her head in the toilet bowl to come home.

He dropped his briefcase, took off his jacket and came into the bathroom with her. "This is the second time this week that you've thrown up. Maybe you should see a doctor."

Angel finished heaving into the toilet, flushed it and then rinsed out her mouth at the sink. "I don't need to see a doctor. DeMarcus and I just got into a big fight and my stomach got upset, that's all."

"What were y'all fighting about?"

Demetrius asked the question. But the look on his face told Angel he already knew. She rushed passed him and closed their bedroom door. She approached her husband with whispered accusations. "You did it, didn't you? You killed him and now the police are going to take you back to jail."

She plopped down on their bed. "What were you thinking, Demetrius? We need you here; not in prison." She beat on her chest, "defending your woman's honor."

Demetrius sat on the bed next to her. He took her hand in his, "I swear to you, Angel. I did not kill Frankie. I wanted to. I even went to his house the moment I was released from jail. But he was already dead."

Looking into Demetrius' eyes told her everything she wanted to know. She believed him. Sighing in relief, she admitted. "I'm not sorry he's dead. The only thing I'm sorry about is that DeMarcus was watching the news when Frankie's death was announced. He knows we lied to him, Demetrius."

Demetrius waved her concern off. "He'll get over it, Angel. I mean, dead is dead. No matter which way or when it comes."

"Yeah, but DeMarcus is angry because I never let him see that scum while he was alive. But we did the right thing by DeMarcus, and nobody will ever convince me of anything different."

"My father has done so much dirt to me and I always turn back around to forgive him." Demetrius went into their walk-in closet and began changing his clothes.

Angel had a problem with Demetrius' statement, because she had come to hate Don Shepherd for what he and Frankie had done to her. She wanted her husband to feel the exact same way, father or not. "What are you saying," Angel asked as she followed Demetrius into the closet. "You're not angry with Don for what happened to me?"

"I was baby… I was real angry."

She folded her arms across her chest. "But you're not angry anymore?"

"It's different for me, Angel. I don't know how to explain it, but I can tell you this… the days that I'm the most angry with my father are days when I look at you and still picture Frankie's hands on you. That's when I wish I could choke 'em both out."

She didn't like hearing that her husband was imaging another man's hands on her, but it was real, so she dealt with it. "And days when you're not so angry… what's going through your mind then."

Demetrius threw on a t-shirt and a pair of shorts. "Those are the days when I remember what I did to him and I remember what he did for us."

"What do you mean?" Angel was asking a question she thought she already knew the answer to, but since Demetrius had yet to confirm her suspicions, she kept them to herself.

He took her hand and moved her back into their bedroom. They sat on the bed again and Demetrius said, "After word got around about what Frankie did to you I was so angry I wanted any and everybody to hurt just the way you and I were hurting. After I talked to you and you told me that my father sent you to Frankie, I assumed that he'd used you just as he'd used my mother all those years ago. So, I told the feds what they wanted to know. And that's why I'm out and he's back in jail, on his way to prison.

"The thought didn't bother me at all... until I saw that knife in Frankie's chest. Then I knew that my father had not sent you to Frankie to be used and abused just so he could get his bond posted."

"How can you say that, Demetrius? You know what happened."

"Yes, but I also know my father. And he wouldn't have killed Frankie if he expected him to do what he did. My father is big on retribution... somebody gets wronged, somebody's got to pay. Simple as that."

Angel nodded as it was sinking in. "So he made Frankie pay for what he did to me?"

"And I made Don pay for all of it. So, forgive me if I sometimes feel a little guilty about what I did to my father after discovering what he'd done for us."

She pulled her husband into an embrace. "I'm sorry Demetrius, I know this has been just as hard on you as it's been on me. But we're going to get through this... you and me."

"It's you and me against the world now, baby. So we don't have no choice but to get through it."

~~~~

But the next morning when Angel jumped out of bed and raced to the bathroom to throw up again. Demetrius walked up behind her and said, "You're pregnant."

"Demetrius, I am not pregnant." Angel rinsed out her mouth and then tried to get around her husband so she could get back in bed, but he wouldn't move out of her way.

"I'm going to the drugstore to buy you a pregnancy test. If it comes back positive, I'm going to make an appointment at the clinic so you can get rid of it."

"Get rid of it?" Angel's eyes just about popped out of her head. "What if it's the little girl that you've been begging me to have the last few years?"

He pointed towards her stomach as if it was the object of his disdain. "I'm not raising Frankie's kid." He turned away from her to throw on a jogging suit.

"You're already raising Frankie's kid. He's in the other room, not speaking to either one of us because he thinks we're a bunch of liars."

"DeMarcus is my son… always has been. But whatever that is," he pointed at her stomach again and then put on his socks and shoes while saying, "I don't want no parts of it."

"Be reasonable, Demetrius. If I am pregnant, the baby could just as well be yours. As a matter-of-fact, there's more of a chance that this is your child than you-know-who." She didn't even want to say his name at this point.

"I've only been home a little over a week Angel. I was locked up for a few weeks. I get home and all of a sudden after years of not getting pregnant again… Dontae is six… and now you're pregnant. I just don't like the odds and I'm not playing Russian roulette."

Demetrius left the house and drove two blocks over to the nearest pharmacy. He threw two pregnancy tests on the counter and pulled his wallet out preparing to pay for them. The clerk looked at him and said, "Dang, as mad as you look, I hope she's not pregnant."

131

"Me too," Demetrius answered as he paid for the kits and then left the store. Rushing back to his car, Demetrius was caught off guard by the sight of Al leaning against his car.

"You picked the wrong day, Al. I'm not in the mood."

"Your father wants to see you... you do remember him, don't you Judas?"

Demetrius tried to ignore him. He unlocked the car door and grabbed for the handle. But Al laid hands on him and threw him against the car. "You better thank your lucky stars that Don loves his only son, because if it was up to me, I would be putting a bullet in you right now."

The bag Demetrius was holding dropped as he said, "I don't have time for this right now, Al."

"You little turn-coat. You've got time for whatever I say you've got time for. Now, I said that your father wants to see you. When should I tell him to expect you?"

"I'll go see him. There, are you happy now?"

Al shook his head. "I won't be happy until you get what's coming to you. It's just too bad that I can't be the one to give it to you." Al backed off, picked up the bag Demetrius dropped and handed it to him. But the bag broke and the pregnancy kits fell out. Al caught one before it hit the ground. He looked at the box and then up at Demetrius.

Demetrius snatched the box out of his hand and then grabbed the other. He threw the kits in the backseat of his car and then got in without saying another word to the man.

When he arrived home, Angel was sitting up in bed, tapping her index finger to her upper lip as if she was trying to figure a way out of this nightmare situation. "Look baby, I understand that you're upset. I would be too. But we can't go jumping to conclusions. What if we're wrong?"

He threw the kits on the bed, and then pointed to the bathroom. "Let's just see how wrong I am."

Staring at Demetrius for a long moment, Angel was the first to break eye contact. She picked up the boxes and went into the bathroom. It took twenty minutes for her to re-open the bathroom door and come out to face her husband. Tears flowed down her face as she told him, "I'm pregnant."

Eighteen

Days after getting a positive on both pregnancy tests Demetrius had brought home, she noticed that her husband was getting home later and later; and that he was choosing to sleep in the guest room rather than in their bedroom.

One night she went to him and said, "Please come back to our bed, Demetrius."

Demetrius sat on the edge of his bed, looking at her as if she was bothering him. "You cancelled the appointment I made you."

Leaning against the doorpost, Angel wrapped her arms around her stomach. "This is not an easy decision for me, Demetrius. You may have grown up with a father who kills just as easily as he changes his shoes. But my family isn't like that. I was raised to believe all life is sacred to God. So, how can I just take the life of my own child?"

"It's not a life yet, Angel. And abortion is legal, it's not murder."

The look on his face clearly showed Demetrius' frustration with her, but Angel had to make him understand where she was coming from. "This country can dress it up any way they like... call a baby a fetus... tell everyone that it's not a life until the murder deems it to be a life and all that nonsense. But the truth of the matter is, a baby is a life from the moment it is conceived. We don't know what this baby is meant to become in this world. Do you really want to destroy a baby that has done nothing to us?"

Demetrius got off the bed, slowly walked over to Angel and then closed the door in her face. She cried all the way up the stairs and threw herself onto her bed. Why was this happening to them? Why was Demetrius forcing her to choose?

After crying herself to sleep, Angel woke the next morning in total despair. She went down to the kitchen to fix breakfast for her family, but Demetrius informed her that he was taking his boys out for the day.

"So you're not even going to allow them to eat breakfast with me?"

"You already have a kid to eat breakfast with. Didn't you tell me that what's in your stomach is alive?"

Turning off the stove, she tried to appeal to the heart that had once beat for her… she prayed that it still did. "I don't want to fight with you, Demetrius. I've loved you so long and I've given you all of me from the moment we got together. Treating me this way is killing me, can't you see that?"

"And what do you think your deciding to have another man's baby is doing to me?"

"You don't know that this baby belongs to Frankie. And I can't destroy a child that belongs to us."

"What if it doesn't belong to us… then what?"

"Then we'll love him just like we love DeMarcus."

"That's different." Demetrius walked over to her, whispered in her ear. "Frankie stole a part of you from me. And now you expect me to just go like it didn't happen and raise his baby. I won't do it, Angel."

"None of this would have happened if you hadn't been lying to me about your dealings with your father's drug business."

"What does that have to do with anything?"

She started counting off. "You got arrested... then you got hurt in jail and I thought you'd get killed in there, so then your father convinced me to go see Frankie. But if you'd gotten a legitimate job like I asked you to do in the first place, you never would have been arrested in the first place... right?"

Demetrius wasn't trying to hear that. "I'd like to know what kind of job you think I could have gotten without a college education that would have allowed you to stay home with these kids all these years... we needed my father. And you turned a blind eye to what was going on because you didn't want to know. So, don't get on your high horse now that the truth has come out."

"That's not fair, Demetrius, because I don't need this big house in order to love you. I don't care where we are or what we have... as long as we have each other."

Demetrius turned dark cold eyes on Angel. He grabbed her with one and squeezed her arm. "I'm warning you, Angel. If you don't abort that baby, you'll regret it."

"You're hurting me." Angel snatched her arm from his grip and rubbed it.

Looming over her as he pointed in her face, Demetrius spat out, "I won't be made a fool of by Frankie Day, you or anybody else. I said, get rid of it and that's what I mean."

As Demetrius stormed out of the kitchen Angel sat at the table too stunned to move. Since the night he snatched her away from Frankie, she'd always thought of him as her savior, her protector. But for the first time since knowing Demetrius, she actually feared him and worried about what he might do if she didn't obey him.

Demetrius didn't say another word to her as he got the kids dressed. Her sons didn't even come into the kitchen to give her a hug or kiss before Demetrius rushed them out of the house. She was becoming a piranha in her own home. Angel touched her stomach as tears rolled down her eyes. "What if this is our baby?"

~~~~

Demetrius met with his father in a small room just outside the visitation room. Don walked in, the handcuffs were taken off of him; he then whispered something to the guard.

The guard then turned to Demetrius and said, "I'll be right outside, just knock on the door if you need me." As he opened the door, he turned back to them and said, "You've got five minutes."

"Got 'em all rolling over and doing your bidding in here too, huh?" Demetrius wanted to laugh, but his life was too sad right now.

"Every man has to feed his family," Don told him.

"Well, you've got me here in this cushy room, rather than meeting with me where the rest of the prisoners visit, so now what? You plan on giving me some street justice for what I did?"

"I understand your anger son, Al told me about the pregnancy test." Don closed his eyes for a moment, then went on and asked, "Is she?"

Demetrius' lip curled. "Yeah… isn't that just great."

"What are you going to do?"

"I'm not keeping it, if that's what you're asking."

Don nodded as if his son was doing the right thing. Then he scooted his chair closer to Demetrius and lowered his voice. "The reason I needed to see you is because your life is in danger."

"Yeah, I know," Demetrius said, "You're going to have Al kill me."

"Listen to me Son, I am a nightmare to many men. But I am not your nightmare. I would never deliberately harm you. And I'd make anyone pay, if they dared to harm you. But even your daddy can't stop the train that's coming at you. So I suggest you pay close attention to what I'm about to tell you."

"Why would you help me, when I'm the reason you're back in jail?"

"I know that you hate me. And maybe you have good reason. But I still need to protect my family. You see, I've never talked to you about the men I do business with because I didn't want you involved."

"I already know that you and your boys don't trust me, and maybe y'all were right for that," Demetrius said as he lowered his head.

"I'm not talking about trust... the men I deal with are some real bad dudes. They're Columbians, Demetrius. Do you know what that means?"

When Demetrius didn't respond, Don continued, "It means that they aren't going to take a loss without somebody getting killed. Why do you think I started ordering more from them after Michael Crane got killed... they demanded it."

"What are you talking about... they demanded it? I've never known you to take orders from anybody."

"I can't control the Columbians, Demetrius. So, here's what you are going to do. When they come to see you----"

"Wait." Demetrius did the time out sign with his hand. "Why you think they coming after me."

"Because that's how they operate. You rolled on me and now I'm not on the street running drugs for them. They will want to make you pay for that and they will kill Angel and the kids too."

"Why did you even start dealing with people like this in the first place?"

"Because I wanted in at the top, so I made as many deals with the devil as I had to. But I never involved you… now you're involved. So, when they come to see you, tell them that I have authorized you to take over as the head of our organization. Tell them that you are working out a way to receive their next shipment."

"I'm not a drug dealer. I'm a businessman." Demetrius had his chest puffed out, but Don deflated it.

"I made you a businessman and now you're going to get your hands dirty with the true family business. Because if you don't, none of us will survive."

~~~~

Behold, *One* sat on the throne in heaven. And He who sat there was like a sparkling precious stone in appearance; and *there was* a rainbow around the throne, in appearance like an emerald. Around the throne *were* twenty-four thrones, and on the thrones I saw twenty-four elders sitting, clothed in white robes; and they had crowns of gold on their heads. And from the throne proceeded lightning, thundering, and voices. Seven lamps of fire *were* burning before the throne, which are the seven Spirits of God.

Before the throne *there was* a sea of glass, like crystal. And in the midst of the throne, and around the throne, *were* four living creatures full of eyes in front and in back. The first living creature *was* like a lion, the second living creature like a calf, the third living creature had a face like a man, and the fourth living creature *was* like a flying eagle. *The* four living creatures, each having six wings, were full of eyes around and within. And they do not rest day or night, saying:

"Holy, holy, holy,

Lord God Almighty,

Who was and is and is to come!"

Whenever the living creatures give glory and honor and thanks to Him who sits on the throne, who lives forever and ever, the twenty-four elders fall down before Him who sits on the throne and worship Him who lives forever and ever, and cast their crowns before the throne, saying:

"You are worthy, O Lord,

To receive glory and honor and power;

For You created all things,

And by Your will they exist and were created."

Then Captain Aaron and Saul bowed down and praised the Lord. The general, Arch Angel Michael lifted up their heads and then brought them before the throne. Then the voice of thunder and lightning commanded them.

Saul took out his sword and lifted it high. "I will fight for the baby's life with all that is in me."

Nineteen

KeKe didn't have to get out of bed for another hour in order to get her children ready for school and then get over to the restaurant to set the place up for next week's opening. But there was a tugging in her spirit, and she couldn't stay in bed. She got on her knees and started bombarding heaven with prayers for Angel. She hadn't seen her friend in over a week because Demetrius demanded that she spend her time getting the restaurant set up rather than bothering his wife.

She didn't understand why Demetrius was so hateful to her when they had once been so cool. But KeKe didn't hold it against him, she just lifted Demetrius up in prayer every chance she got. But this morning her prayers were all for Angel. "Lord, I don't know what's wrong... if she's still depressed over what Frankie did to her or if she and Demetrius are having problems, but please, please help Angel. Be with her today. Give her a heart to hear from You. Lead my friend closer and closer to You so that she can find peace."

KeKe wasn't the only one who was woken out of her sleep, Maxine got out of bed early that morning as well. She warmed a cup of coffee and then went onto the back patio to spend a little time with Jesus. Her daughter had been heavily on her heart and mind ever since they came to visit last month. It had been a shocker to discover that DeMarcus was not Demetrius' son as Angel had told them for so many years. But Maxine wasn't condemning her daughter for that. Like the bible says, 'all have sinned and come short of the glory of God.

What bothered Maxine was that Angel still didn't feel like she could come to them. She and Marvin messed up their kids' lives a long time ago when they themselves had allowed sin to reign in their home, now they would have to take on this fight and get their daughter back.

The door opened and Marvin peeked his head out. "I couldn't sleep without you next to me. Why are you on the patio so early?" It was six in the morning.

"We need to pray for Angel. We need to stay on our knees until that girl receives her breakthrough. We owe her that much." Maxine told her husband, and the angel who'd been massaging her temples causing her to remember the things that caused Angel to lose her faith in the first place, smiled… mission accomplished.

~~~~

The day finally came when Angel could take no more. She desperately wanted her husband to love her and for her family to be the tight knit unit they'd once been. And she just wasn't strong enough to fight Demetrius one more day. So she got in her car and drove down to the clinic on the east side of town, hoping that she wouldn't run into anyone that she knew.

She pulled into the lot and checked the time. Her appointment was scheduled for 9 a.m. She was twenty minutes early, so she sat in her car and took a few deep breaths. Taking the key out of the ignition, Angel looked out at the street and that's when she noticed the people holding picket signs.

One sign said, 'Don't Kill Your Baby… Every Life Matters. Then another sign had on it, 'Jeremiah 1:5'.

The scripture was not written on that poster, but it didn't have to be. It was the same scripture her father used to read to her when she was a child: *Before I formed you in the womb I knew you; Before you were born I sanctified you.*

As the words of Jeremiah shocked her system, Angel once again realized why she thought of abortion as murder. Because if God knew a child and could sanctify him or her before they were even born, then the so-called fetus had to be a living thing. Angel was undone. All she had done was love a man who loved her and their family more than anything else. But life had dealt them a blow and now she didn't know what to do, didn't know how to choose right rather than wrong.

Tears were blurring her eyes as the woman who'd been holding the 'Every Life Matters' poster knocked on her door. Angel wiped her face and rolled down the window.

The woman asked, "Would you like to talk to someone?"

Angel nodded as she unlocked the door and allowed the woman to get in the car.

The woman extended her hand. "I'm Patricia Miller-Harding. You don't have to cry anymore because God sent me here for you."

"Why would God send you to me?"

"You don't believe me?" Patricia put a gentle hand on Angel's shoulder as she said, "I know everything about you, Angel."

"How do you know my name?"

"God has given me a glimpse into your life… I know that your upbringing was all about the Lord and growing closer to Him. Until your parent's divorce, you had even planned to go into the ministry yourself. But then you ran away, moved in with a street-wise guy, and when he tossed you out, instead of humbling yourself and going back to your parents, who had re-married, you started stripping and then you fell in love with another criminal. You married him and now he has you here, about to kill one of God's soldiers."

"Who are you?" were the only words Angel could form. She was stunned that this woman could so read her. What was going on?

"I'm a friend, sent by the Lord with a message for you."

"What's the message," Angel asked, still feeling a little devastated by the way she'd just been read.

Patricia looked directly into Angel's eyes and held onto her hands as she said, "Thus says the Lord, you were born to serve God, you chose not to… but this baby you are carrying will not be swayed by the enemy. He will do great and mighty things for the Lord."

Angel bowed her head as tears rolled down her face. When she was a little girl, she used to stand behind a makeshift podium, preaching her heart out to the kids in the neighborhood. Her dad had told her that God had a calling on her life. She had believed it then. But when her dad hadn't been able to hold onto his own calling, Angel let hers slip away.

As she grew older Angel began to think that so much more was out there in the world, and that she was missing out on the good life by serving the Lord. But in truth, she had left the good life and was now suffering dearly for it. But her children didn't have to suffer, and they could grow to be much better human beings than she and Demetrius ever dreamed of being.

Angel turned her attention back to Patricia. She seemed like such a God fearing woman and her eyes were kind. So, Angel prayed that she could answer one question for her… because the answer to this question would solve all of her problems. "God has told you all this stuff about me, right?"

Patricia smiled. "The Lord loves you."

She wanted to scream at Patricia, then where was he when Frankie attacked me? But instead she asked, "Then tell me this, is the baby I'm carrying Demetrius' son?"

Without hesitation, Patricia told her, "The baby you're carrying will grow to be a great man of God. And God shall be his father."

That was an awesome thing for her child, but it still wasn't the answer she needed.

Patricia then said, "Go see KeKe, she is waiting at her house for you with another message from the Lord." The woman then got out of her car and disappeared.

It was 9 o'clock, time for Angel's appointment. But she couldn't get out of the car. Demetrius would hate her for this, but she wasn't going to kill her baby. She was going to birth him, love and care for him and sit back and wait to see the man he turned out to be. Pulling away from the abortion clinic, Angel headed for KeKe's place.

When she arrived, she got out of her car and slowly walked to her friend's door. She hadn't told KeKe about the baby, so she didn't know how she was going to broach the subject about whether or not she had a word from the Lord for her. Because Angel certainly wasn't going to admit that she had run into a woman at an abortion clinic.

Before she could knock on the door, KeKe swung it open. Her keys were in her hand. "Angel, what are you doing here?"

"Are you going somewhere?" Angel asked, avoiding the question.

"I'm headed back to the restaurant. I drove all the way down there this morning, but forgot the key to unlock the door, so I had to come back home to get them."

Was it just a coincidence that KeKe had come back home and that Angel had arrived to her house right before she left again? Angel didn't know what was going on, but God had finally gotten her attention. She silently prayed, "Lord, lead and guide me. I'm ready to follow You again. Just tell me what You want me to do."

At that moment KeKe snapped her finger as if she had forgotten something. "It's funny that you showed up here this morning, because I was going to come by your house when I finished working tonight."

"Really, what for?"

"I was reading in my bible this morning and the strangest thing happened. I know you probably won't believe me, but it felt like an angel directed me to a passage that was meant just for you."

"You'd be surprised," Angel told her. "Do you mind showing me that passage?"

Angel and KeKe stepped into the house. KeKe grabbed her bible and opened it to Exodus 34:10 and began to read: "*Behold, I make a covenant. Before all your people I will do marvels such as have not been done in all the earth, nor in any nation; and all the people among whom you shall see the work of the Lord. For it is an awesome thing that I will do with you.*"

"What does it mean?" KeKe asked once she finished reading, but Angel couldn't answer her because she was on the floor bowed down, praising God and giving Him all the glory for what He was about to do in her life.

"God is good… God is good," Angel kept saying over and over again. She wasn't afraid anymore. She knew what she had to do and where her loyalties must lie from this moment forward.

KeKe got down on the floor with her. She held onto Angel's hands as she asked, "You're ready to come back to the Lord, aren't you?"

Tears blurred Angel's vision as she told her friend, "I need the Lord in my life. I can't live another day without Him."

"Then raise your hands and repeat after me."

Angel lifted her hands and began repeating, "Jesus is the Son of God... He died and rose again so that I could be saved..."

When they finished praying, Angel hugged KeKe and she told her. "I was so wrong."

"God has got you right now, so don't worry about the past."

"No, I mean, I was wrong about you. When you first showed up at my house, I thought you needed my help, God knew that I was the one who needed help... thank you for being here for me."

On the drive home, Angel was amazed that she didn't feel any fear for what Demetrius might say or do when she told him that she didn't go through with the abortion. She trusted God, and believed that He was well able to change Demetrius' heart.

When she was about five minutes away from the house, Demetrius called. She was tempted to ignore his call so that she'd have just a little more time to bask in the glory of her new found joy. But after the third ring, she decided to face the music.

The moment she answered, Demetrius was screaming through the phone, "Where are you?"

Did he already know that she hadn't followed his orders? "I'm on my way home."

"So, you're not in the house?" he was still shouting.

"No. What's wrong?"

"The kids at school?"

"Yes, Demetrius, the kids are at school. What's going on?"

"The house is on fire."

Angel was at a stop light. "What!"

"Go get the kids and drive them to your mother's house. I'll wire some money down there so you can get them some clothes."

She pulled into a parking lot, shaking her head. "Why do we have to leave you? Why can't we just stay here and look for another place?"

"It's not safe here, Angel. Just get the kids and get out of here. I'll let you know what's going on later. But we don't have time to play around."

"But we need to talk. I have some things to tell you." Angel tried.

"We'll talk later. Just go."

He hung up on her without letting her tell him about the baby or about her salvation experience. She wanted to stay here with Demetrius no matter what was going on, but she had to protect her children and the baby that was growing inside of her.

~~~

Demetrius wanted to get in his truck and follow his family, but the Columbian had visited him this morning. He had told them that he would not become their lackey... drugs was not his thing and he wanted no part of it. They'd left his office without saying a word. Then he received the call that his house was on fire. He had to protect his family and to do that Demetrius would have to take over for his father. He doubted that Angel would ever forgive him for what he was about to do, but somebody had to keep their family alive.

As Demetrius stood in front of his house staring at the flames that engulfed his home, Saul stood next to him. It had been Saul's job to convince Angel to leave town. Because the child must be born in a

148

house where God is continually being praised. He must also be baptized and only then can he be returned to this land of sin and ill-gotten gain.

The end of Book II

Stay tuned for Book III, Love and Honor coming in August 2016

Don't forget to join my mailing list:
http://vanessamiller.com/events/join-mailing-list/
Join me on Facebook: https://www.facebook.com/groups/
77899021863/
Join me on Twitter: https://www.twitter.com/vanessamiller01

Family Business

Book 1

Sample Chapter

Family Business Series

One

Ten years later...

"Let me go, Frankie. I'm done with this job and I'm done with you," a woman was yelling as Demetrius and Mo made their way up the alley.

Demetrius was thankful for the noise because it was leading him straight to the man they came to see. As they rounded the corner and rolled up on Frankie Day, Demetrius firmly held the bat that he used to practice with.

Frankie gripped the woman's arm with one hand and smacked her across the face with the other.

"I don't care if you beat me," the woman yelled. "Do whatever you want, but you're not going to make a whore out of me."

Demetrius couldn't see the girl's face because as they rounded the corner, they were facing Frankie's back and she was directly in front of him. But there was no fear in her voice, even after being struck hard. And Demetrius knew what fear sounded like. He'd heard it often enough from men who were supposed to be tough guys. But the minute he unleashed his beat down, things changed.

"You a stripper, Angel. You act like I'm asking you to do something you ain't never heard of."

"I won't do it," she said.

Frankie shoved her and then lifted a fist, getting ready to strike her again, but that's when Demetrius grabbed Frankie's arm and swung him around. "Didn't your mama tell you that boys aren't supposed to hit girls?"

Frankie's fist balled so he could strike out at the intruder. But once he caught sight of Demetrius, he backed up. "Hey man, you coming out to see my girls tonight...drinks on me."

As Demetrius grabbed Frankie, Mo held onto the woman, making sure she didn't run off and warn any of Frankie's boys. But somehow, Demetrius doubted that she wanted to help Frankie. He glanced over at her, and for a minute he almost forgot why he was in the alley in the first place. It was her eyes... big, brown and sexy, Even sexier than that white teddy and that see-it-all robe she was wearing. That caramel coated skin and long flowing sandy colored hair went well with those eyes and that teddy.

Demetrius pulled his eyes away from her, trying hard to focus as he told Frankie, "Can't come in tonight. Daddy's got me here on business." He then lifted the bat and smacked it into his free hand.

"Don don't have nothing to worry about with me. Business is good. I'll have his money by the end of the night." Frankie then turned to the vision in white and said, "If I could stop chasing these runaway strippers."

From the conversation Demetrius overheard as they walked up, it sounded like Frankie wanted this girl to do more than just strip.

"I'm not running away, I quit," she said with fire in those brown eyes.

"You don't get to quit on me. I own you in more ways than one." He poked a finger at her chest. "Remember that."

She tried to spit on him, but Frankie moved out of the way and then leaped on her like he thought the boys were there to watch him deliver a beat down. But Demetrius wasn't having it. Frankie got off a right-handed blow to the woman's cheek, but then Demetrius swung that bat like he was going for a home run. Frankie yelled and then fell to the ground.

"Why'd you stop me? I'm trying to get her in line so I can earn the money I owe your daddy."

"We came here to beat you down, not watch you beat some defenseless woman." Demetrius was about to swing again.

Frankie lifted his hands while sitting up and scooting back against the brick wall of his strip club. "Don't do this Demetrius, I got the money."

Demetrius really wanted to keep pounding this fool. But if he beat Frankie rather than collect the money his father sent him after, then he'd have to deal with Don Shepherd and nobody in their organization wanted to deal with his daddy. "Where's the money?"

"That-that's what I been trying to tell you. I got ten thou." Frankie stood back up, but kept a distance between him and Demetrius. He pointed towards the vision in white. "And one of my VIPs is ready to give me the other five right now if Angel will spend the night with him. He's crazy about her, and is upstairs waiting while she's down here giving me attitude."

The girl's name was Angel. She looked like an angel, Demetrius thought to himself. Too sweet and pure to be getting beat down in an alley because she didn't want to be pimped out. Or maybe this was a regular fight Frankie and Angel had every week. Maybe she just didn't like the john who was so hot for her. "She can make five G's in one night?" Demetrius asked incredulously.

"I'm telling you, man, this dude has been begging to have Angel for months now. Angel don't go in for stuff like that so I've been saying no." He hunched his shoulders. "But I got this debt with your daddy. So, it's time for Angel to help me out for once in her life."

Demetrius glanced over at Angel, tears were streaming down her face. He turned back to Frankie and said, "You got the ten G's on you now?"

Frankie pointed behind him, indicating the strip club which was nothing more than an old house, turned into a speakeasy/strip club. "In my safe. I was going to bring it around later tonight once I collected the rest of the money."

Demetrius directed Mo to go into the club with Frankie and collect the money. He then told them, "I'll stay right here with the money maker."

As Frankie and Mo headed inside, Demetrius eyed Angel from head to toe and back again. She was a vision of loveliness. Easily one the most beautiful girls Demetrius had seen in a long while. Other women might have been more polished. But the girl standing before him had a few more years to go before anyone would ever consider her a full-grown woman. By then, Demetrius figured she'd outshine any woman. Even Diahann Carroll back in her day. "How old are you?"

"I'm almost nineteen?" she answered while wiping the tears from her face.

"So, you're eighteen." Demetrius shook his head. "Why aren't you at home, letting your mama teach you how to cook, so you can land a husband or something?"

Restoring her tough girl exterior, Angel told him, "I'm going to mind my own business, and let you do the same."

"Oh, Okay." Demetrius put his hands up, indicating he was backing off. "Alright Ms. Mind-my-own-business. You don't seem to be doing such a good job of that, seeing as how you were just being slapped around in this alley."

"What do you know about it?"

Demetrius sat down on the stoop. "I might not know much about your situation, but if it was me, I sure wouldn't be in this alley when Frankie returned."

"I can't just leave."

Demetrius' eye brow lifted. He didn't understand this woman. Maybe she was just pretending that turning tricks bothered her. After all, she was a stripper... already getting paid for showing it, why not sell it all. "Hey, I tried to offer you a way out of this mess, but if you don't want to take it and run... then I'm going to sit over here and mind my own business like you suggested."

Angel glanced around the alley as if trying to find a way out. Her feet shuffled, then she turned to Demetrius and said, "I do want to go, but his sister babysits my kid. If I don't do what Frankie wants, he'll never let my baby go."

The tears were back, and even though she wiped them away quickly, Demetrius' heart was melting for her. It was like he wasn't seeing Angel, but his own mother, desperate to get out of a life that would kill her and take her away from him. He wasn't going to let another child endure the same pain he endured because some low-life decided to treat his mother like she was nothing and could be handled any kind of way.

"Okay, here it is," Frankie said as he and Mo came back into the alley. He handed Demetrius a stack of cash. "Count it if you want, but it's all there."

"Not all," Demetrius said as he pointed toward Angel. "We still need that five thou."

"Problem with that," Frankie kept his eyes on Demetrius' bat as he said, "Dude got tired of waiting and left. But if you give me another week, I'll make sure that Angel works overtime to get that money."

"I'm not working another second for you. I just want to get my son and I'll be on my way."

Frankie reared back, getting ready to hit Angel again, but Demetrius grabbed his arm. "I told you already that we didn't come here to watch you beat on some woman."

Frustrated Frankie said, "Don wants his money. I'm trying to get it for him."

"I think I can help you out with that," Demetrius said. "I'll take the money you just gave me to my dad and then we will clear the books."

"Just like that?" Frankie asked in a tone that indicated he didn't believe Demetrius. "You're just going to forget about that other five?"

"Yeah, it's forgotten, no problem." Demetrius then pointed at Angel and said, "but I want her." He kept his eye on her as if she were a prize that he was bound and determined to win.

"What do you mean… for the night?"

Demetrius shook his head, still staring at Angel. "For good. This is her last night working for you anyway. So, from now on, she's with me."

"Now hold on, Demetrius. Angel is worth a lot more to me than five thou. The most I could do is rent her out to you for about a week. That's it."

Demetrius shook his head. "Take it or leave it. But just know that once I leave, you will be dealing with Don from here on out." He signaled for Mo to follow him, and twirled his bat as he headed out of the alley.

Mo caught up with him and whispered, "Don is gon' be ticked about this. We can't leave here without breaking an arm or a leg at least."

"I got this," Demetrius silenced Mo.

They kept walking, while Demetrius silently counted down "... 5... 4... 3... 2..."

"Hold up," Frankie called out to him. "Go on and take her, she ain't been nothing but trouble to me lately."

Angel didn't move, she looked from Demetrius to Frankie, as if she was unsure which devil would do her the most harm.

Then Demetrius said. "Come on Angel, I'll take you to pick up your son."

Angel still didn't move, she turned to Frankie, her eyes seemed to plead with him, "Can I take DeMarcus?"

Frankie glared at her with hatred building in his eyes. He practically spat at her as he said, "I don't care what you do, just don't come crawling back here once Demetrius is through with you."

He didn't have to tell her twice. Angel rushed over to Demetrius and got in the passenger seat while Mo climbed in the back.

Driving down the street, Mo told Demetrius, "I don't like this, man. Heads are going to roll when we get back to Don. He is not going to like that you bought some chick rather than collecting the rest of his money."

"This ain't on you, Mo. I can handle Don... besides, he owes me one."

~~~~~

Saul's hawking form glided over the alley. He had one assignment for the night and it had been completed. Now he turned his big flapping wings and went up, up, up until he reached his heavenly home. As his feet touched down, his wings closed and his bejeweled sword could be seen as it hung from the belt strapped to his waist all the way to the tip of his foot.

Heaven had three parts, the inner court, the outer court and the Holy of holies where the throne of God resides. Saul made his way to the outer court where Captain Aaron stood in the midst of legions of angels, sending some out and welcoming others back home. Saul saluted his captain and then announced, "It is done my Captain. The two have met."

"Now the hard work begins," Captain Aaron told him.

"And these two are meant to be together?" Saul questioned. from what he saw of them, it seemed like a train wreck. But he wasn't God Almighty, so he didn't have any answers for the fallen humans.

"You may not have the answers," Captain Aaron said, cutting into Saul's thoughts. "But the child that will know both the truth of God and the ways of the street. He shall not only bring his family to Christ, but he shall be the one to usher in the last day revival, that will rock a nation and bring more souls to Christ than any other revolution the world has ever known."

"I do not understand it, my Captain, but I am your willing servant. You tell me where to go and what to do and I will protect these two with everything I've got."

"You have fought and won many battles, Saul. But, even you will need help with this assignment. You see, the child's life will be in danger even before he is born. The battle will be great, but if you and the other angels are able to dispatch the enemy, then revival will come to a nation that greatly needs it."

"And if we don't… I can't imagine the world getting any worse than it is now."

Captain Aaron put a hand on Saul's shoulder. "It will get much worse, my friend. So, you must protect Angel and Demetrius. And when it is time, protect the child, Tolbert, until the very end; for he shall proclaim the truth of God."

Lifting his sword, Saul pledged, "I will fight, and we will win; you have my word, Captain."

Family Business I is available in Print and ebook…

CPSIA information can be obtained
at www.ICGtesting.com
Printed in the USA
LVOW04s1457141016

508817LV00009B/718/P